A WALK IN THE RAIN

Ernest O. Izedonmwen

PAGE PUBLISHING, INC.
New York, NY

First originally published by Page Publishing, Inc. 2018

This is entirely a work of fiction. Any resemblances to any person (living or dead) character or event, except as to names of countries and cities are purely coincidental.

Cover Design:
Concept: Author
Graphics: Uyi, (my son) a budding economist with huge talent

ISBN 978-1-64350-789-7 (Paperback)
ISBN 978-1-64350-790-3 (Digital)

Printed in the United States of America

To my wife, Adesuwa, and my children, Osasere Lexley, Osasuyi Alex, Esosa Naomi, and Jeffrey Nosa.

AND

To the "Chibok Women" for surviving War and Peace.

Acknowledgements

As my publication coordinator, Courtney (Reefer) Winder, will attest this note has been the most difficult part of this book haven been subjected to numerous reviews and revisions. She endured and embraced my impertinence with the type of winks, nods, and enthusiasms of one used to herding unruly teens. Of course, her task was not made any lighter by the absolute and perfect technological ignorance of the author. Consequently, I received several emails attempting to explain the various esoteric details of adobe attachments, (PDF not the political party), cookies, etc. This is my convoluted way of saying thank you Ms. Courtney.

Also, quite unexpectedly, writing an acknowledgment proved intractably difficult, because of the unrestrained vastness of the subject. In the array of people, places, events, inanimate objects and things that have crossed my life, which of these deserve a mention here, without becoming, in "WS" speak **"a tale told by an idiot...."**

As the great German Philosopher, Martin Heidegger, would have put it, even hospital beds provide unique perspectives. Thus, my profound gratitude to my invincible mustache for providing a default latch, when I hit the proverbial writer's block, while my steaming and hardly sipped cup of black tea foams its assurance that the prodigal idea or word will return to a grateful author.

Now, I turn to the most travelled road yet lacking the safety net of a loud orchestra ushering me off the stage with "Hit the road Jack...", my family—to my wife Adesuwa (Mama Lin); and children; Lexley (Red); Alex (Baba); Esosa (Mama Dodoo) and Nosa (Jefito) thanks for everything.

Also, to my cousin, Godfrey (Guflto), an early convert who in grammar school, class 3A, upon reading a pre-publication article I wrote for the school "Newspaper" titled "The Stones We Eat HAVE TOO Many Rice!", concluded that "I" will be famous someday. Thanks bro. The article however, earned me a two-week suspension at the School garden, with "HARD LABOR."

To the following people who appear only in sobriquets perhaps to avoid the embarrassment of any public association with this book: PSK, Mama EJ, Alhaja, Chig, Toyin (Anto). These folks read it when the author could not afford a typewriter but offered them "A FIRST OF AIR" – as the book was then known, written in long hand on yellow pads with no word processor to create the illusion of instant perfection. Please pick up your Jack Robinson Awards—John Oshodi, Ola. Anyanwu, Ikenna, Amaka, Ogechi, Ebele and Zino

Finally, how can I keep from singing your praise– Thank you Lord! And as they say in my other pre–occupation "The Author RESTS!"

1

Osaru slapped himself hard; the pain was sharp and lingering. Mosquito noises was constant and unrelenting throughout the night, but he was too tired to swat any. This one was particularly tenacious, it hung around long enough to rouse him. Slowly, he came to consciousness but his head had a slow but persistent throbbing pain. He held his head in his palms as if to reassure himself that his skull was not splitting open. His body was wet and aching. It was early morning, but there were beads of sweat on his brow. Slowly, he traced the antecedents of his crapulent state.

The committee of friends, as his two close friends called themselves, held a send off party in his honor, but in the usual flamboyant lexicon of his countrymen, they had "thrown a send-off party, which was not just a party but an event!" In point of fact, it was a great party. His mind was fully alert now. He allowed himself to recall the splendor of the previous night. Osaru arrived at the party close to midnight. He made an "entrance," meaning arriving fashionably late. Early arrivals haven "warmed" the party, invited guests arrived late to enjoy themselves free from the infantile enthusiasm of the earlier uninvited "parasites."

Osaru's entrance was tumultuous. The halogen light from the video camera squarely focused on his overly oiled forehead. He was beaming from ear to ear while absorbing the adulation and well-wishes, genuine or perfunctory, like a sponge. The bar would have made the world's largest distillers envious, and Osaru and his guests helped themselves liberally. He was not a discriminatory drinker—

brand, make, kind, warts, and all—but the chemistry of the liquor and his greedy appetite did not make a harmonious mix.

At the end of the day, he had almost spilled out his internal anatomy through his mouth. He could not recall how he got home. The last thing he remembered was being held tightly by his fiancée, Ese. Even then, she was actually two people with the potential of multiplying further. For some strange reason, everybody appeared to be marching backwards. She held on tightly to him, trying to prevent him from doing something that, in his inebriated mind, was perfectly logical, but she would not let him. He learned later that he was attempting to get rid of his trousers!

The party was to send him off to America. He was one of the lucky few who were honored with a six months visiting visa to the United States of America. Six months he reckoned would be enough to build a new life and he was not beyond trying. The United States of America! The land of the dollar. A six-month visiting visa was worth celebrating.

Now, he sat on his bed, hurting, sick to his stomach with a giant-sized headache. The radio jumped to life. It had been on through the night, but the chatter of the host DJ was just going on air. They were advertising some kind of powder. It claimed to cure everything from cancer to pimples. He wished he had some now. He remembered hearing from somewhere that a hangover from drinking could be cured promptly by consuming more alcohol. He was not in the mood for any kind of liquid now. He wondered if that was even an effective remedy or an alcoholic's excuse for perpetual inebriation. Whatever, he had taken his last drink, at least for some time.

Ese turned, muttered something incomprehensible, and was back to asleep. Osaru looked at her. She was so serene. She was dark complexioned, close to polished, glittering ebony, with dreamy eyes always threatening to close; when opened in mock surprise, they revealed a childlike innocence. Her lips were sumptuous, with neatly penciled edges, enclosing an incandescent set of teeth. She was slightly built, but all the curves were in the right places—the hips, the chest fitted with protrusions that stood upright like starched military khakis. She was a second-year pharmacy student at a local university. He could never stop admiring her. She was always there for him. The smartest thing he ever did, he told himself, was getting engaged to her.

Lagos International Airport was an aging pretentious edifice, erected by Nigeria in the hay days of the oil boom. The airport, now a shadow of its former self, still stood defiantly, like an old woman who was once the village beauty. Despite all the evidence of decay and neglect, a careful observer would not fail to notice the architectural masterpiece it once was.

The lounge was teeming with people. His people were naturally vivacious and loquacious. Most discussions were essentially one-up-manship to determine who could shout the loudest. When alcohol was introduced into the mix, as on this occasion, the noise was deafening. Amid the cacophony and comings and goings, the airport looked like a big village market. Business here, however, was different. There were young men and women behind small glass cubicles who looked suspiciously at every document presented to them. They frowned, flipped the documents, and massaged it before certifying it adequate or otherwise. If the passenger passed the scrutiny, he walked back to his family and friends all smiles to continue last-minute rapport. However, when the documents failed to make the grade, there were vigorous arguments resulting in more delays. It was the turn of the man immediately ahead of Osaru to check in. The British Airways booth had a perky, well-put-together woman probably in her early twenties. She appeared to have spent a considerable length of time putting on her makeup. Her efforts were well worth it; she was visible from every part of the lounge. An argument ensued between her and the stocky diminutive man ahead of Osaru. The argument was about the man's "request" ticket. She tried to explain to him that the status of his ticket meant that he could not be guaranteed a seat until other passengers with confirmed tickets had been checked in. She further warned him that getting a seat from Lagos did not guarantee that a seat would be available from London to America. He was indignant at the information. He explained that his booking agent had sworn that he had a confirmed ticket. Unimpressed by his argument, she asked him to step aside and wait or she would call security. He dared her. She obliged him. A fierce-looking soldier with his fingers trained on the trigger of his gun appeared, and our man meekly walked away. The ticket clerk, an ungracious victor shouted after him "I think say you dey crazy. Why you run if your mama born you well." Still gloating from her triumph, it was Osaru's turn. She proceeded with magisterial deliberation. Momentarily, she produced a hand lens to view the visa stamp on the passport closer. There was a worried brow forming now across her face, then she asked, "Where you dey go?"

"Dallas," he blurted out.

"For what?" she asked.

"Visiting."

"Okay, safe journey." The storm gathering in his stomach quickly subsided. Little did he know that this was only the opening salvo in a plethora of battles he was to fight in his checkered sojourn. For now, however, he was relieved and back in the cocoon of family and friends. The moment he had dreaded for a long time was at hand; it was time for final goodbyes, back slaps, and tears.

A line from an old Mahattans song stuck in his mind: "When You Walk Away, Don't Look Back." As he walked into the tunnel that emptied passengers into the belly of the plane, he resisted the urge to look back. If he had, he would have seen that his sister, Ivie, and Ese were in tears. Ese, who was ordinarily phlegmatic, for once shed the cool and calculated exterior and poured out her soul. As Osaru disappeared from view, the reality of the separation settled in on her. He was gone, perhaps forever, the only man she had really grown to love. Her people pejoratively referred to the village beauty betrothed to village chief's son who was "overseas" as an "airport widow." She could visualize now the cruel satisfaction of rejected suitors, with their "I told you so" winks and snickers. Life was unfair, she concluded.

Ivie had always been around her brother all her life. He had just walked off. What if he married an *Oyinbo* (white) woman? He would be lost forever. She was reliably informed that Oyinbo women did not tolerate relatives in their matrimonial home. It was said that you could not visit them without prior invitation! "Invitation only" for relatives was unheard of among his people. You simply showed up and you were welcomed. Oyinbo women were alleged to do something to their husbands which made them forget family and maintain perpetual allegiance to their spouses, like faithful dogs. She would not give up on her only brother without a fight, Oyinbo or whatever woman.

2

Osaru sat in his seat and killed time with magazines tucked in the back pocket of every seat. They were basically the airline industry's newsletters, with glossy pictures and pages. He had been at this a while when a generously proportioned lady came through the aisle, dragging several bags. He wondered how she got past the stern hostess at the door who warned passengers of the two-bag limit for carry-on luggage. Well, some people did not bother with rules; with her size, she probably and perhaps literally bullied her way through any obstacles.

She heaved herself into the seat next to Osaru and promptly went to sleep. Osaru envied her efficiency. There she was a minute ago, hauling several pounds of luggage without breaking a sweat. Now done she wasted not a second on idle chatters or anything else but resting and soundly asleep. Maybe the poor woman was tired, he thought. Who knew? She probably spent the previous night at a party. Maybe she had to fight her way to the airport against demanding relatives, kleptomaniac police officers, greedy soldiers at the numerous checkpoints, and of course, the almost-mandatory verbal war with the ticket clerks.

"In five minutes we shall be landing in Accra, Ghana," a voice announced over the intercom, perhaps the pilot's. He wondered why they had to go through Accra. Accra the capital of Ghana, a neighboring country, but in his opinion, it was an unnecessary forty-minute detour. The airlines were saving cost by combining the routes. Local currencies were hardly worth the paper they were printed on. The airline's action made economic sense, but for someone in a hurry to get to America, it was an inconvenience. Well, America, what were his expectation? Would it live up to billing? Was he setting himself up for failure? No! He rebuked himself and dismissed such thoughts.

America was the land of opportunity; all he ever asked for was an opportunity.

The reputation of airline food preceded it. He had been warned about their quality and quantity. It did not disappoint. For size, everything was miniaturized, and the taste of the chicken sealed his appetite. He was convinced that it was never really cooked.

It was therefore a hungry, tired, and dazed Osaru who landed in London in the early hours of the morning. He was in London! He could not believe it. London was the first city outside his country that registered in his consciousness as a child. As he expected, London was cold and raining. As he looked through the glass walls, umbrellas and long coat appeared to be mandatory dressing code. The airport was ascetically clean. Nothing flashy or bold, just understated elegance. There was a pleasant smell in the air, definitely some kind of food, but he could not tell what it was. It must be delicious, he concluded. Not necessarily, he reversed himself. It was a popular saying among his people that the aroma (actually they call it smell) of a dish does not foretell its taste. He knew that well enough. He was, to put it mildly, not given to culinary excellence, actually not even close to mediocrity, but he knew how to lace his cooking with onions fried in bleached red oil to produce a deceptively seductive aroma. A taste will unmask any pretensions.

The airport had several stores, all displaying their years of establishment like broaches of honor, perhaps for surviving so long in a hostile business environment. The herd mentality was particularly strong here. All shops were identical in more ways than one; they displayed goods in similar fashion, from alcohol to sweaters to cigarettes. The salesgirls looked alike. Their revolving electronic bill boards displayed scantily dressed women hawking their wares. They all proudly announced that they were duty-free. This information apparently made no impact on pricing. Everything carried prohibitive prices, unbelievable to Osaru who converted each price from pounds sterlin (the English currency) to Naira (the Nigerian currency) and was horrified.

He was sitting near a couple who were cuddling like long-lost lovers. They were young and apparently forgot to wash their clothes or cut their hair. The girl had a nose ring. Which Osaru hitherto believed was a primitive ritual in Africa, but incredulously in the heart of heart of London, a white girl with a nose ring—an unlikely example of African Cultural imperialism!

The human traffic at the airport was heavy. People walked briskly and gave the impression of a sense of purpose. Their stern faces and the dour environment depressed him. The people appeared too serious and insular for his taste. In fact, they hardly noticed him. He compared this to the airport he left some hours ago. At home the Airport was just a sophisticated marketplace, boisterous and colorful. Here, the airport was like a column of ants, marching locksteps and carrying on their respective duties with cold efficiency. At home, work was incidental to life; here, it appeared life was incidental to work. He instinctively disliked London. Will America be different?

He ordered sausages and juice. He was sitting alone in the far corner of the airport restaurant. The next table was full. It appeared that the entire genealogical tree was on the move. Among his people, it was considered foolhardy for an entire family to travel together via the same means, the rationale being that a disaster could wipe out the entire family. These folks had no such apprehensions. The eldest male was telling some story, which the eldest female found very amusing. She would cackle and quickly put a handkerchief over her mouth, as if suddenly realizing that it was improper behavior for a lady to laugh so uncontrollably in public, the type his people referred to as "laughing in vernacular." Other members of the group showed polite enthusiasm, but it was obvious that they would rather be listening to something or someone else.

The old man, a determined storyteller, was unhurried and, in an even tone, told his story,

"So the Normans invaded England and stole all the land. These Normans, rascals they were, as new owners, leased the land to the dispossessed owners. The former owners could use the land for a fee, but they could only have an interest in the land, not ownership. Not everybody could afford the new fees. So the idea of landlords or land barons was born. The lords or barons paid the fees for large parcels of land and relet same to the peasantry, who either tilled the land—" Just then the public-address system called on passengers to Frankfurt to board the plane. They jumped with Olympian agility for their flight, relief written all over their faces. Some storyteller.

He still had four hours to kill at the airport. He remembered one of his elementary school principals' constant admonishing aphorism: "Time is money." As a kid, he wondered what it meant. He was of course too scared and timid to ask. Now, however, he knew what the old principal was trying to say. Did the airlines know about this shorthand for efficiency? Why would they keep anybody at an airport for six hours without activities and simply ask them to wait? If time was indeed money, how much was his six hours' worth? Well, the saying presupposed that there was an alternative productive use of his time. So what will he be doing instead? Working in America of course! If he earned sixty dollars for those six wasted hours and converted that to Naira, he would have already squandered a small fortune at the end of six hours! He had to occupy himself somehow, so he placed his medium-sized handheld bag under his seat, ensured it was properly locked, and ventured to take a closer at the airport.

After going through several shops, he bought a novel and planned to completely enmesh himself in it. By the time he got back to his seat at the departure lounge, the entire section had been condoned off by armed security officers with fingers trained on their guns' trigger. He learned on inquiry that security had spotted an unaccompanied bag under a seat. It was airport policy to destroy all unaccompanied bags. It dawned on him that he was the culprit. He watched as the security officers in their extravagant protective gears gingerly carted away his bag. He approached a nearby officer to claim ownership of the bag. He was taken to a small room, where he was interrogated and made to list all contents of the bags. He did the best he could; they were mainly odds and ends—toothpaste, combs and sundry other items. To imagine that these could activate trigger the entire British security forces to full state of alert not seen since the Nazi scourge was surprising and amusing. Eventually, he got his bag back after receiving a stern lecture on the severity of his offense. Thereafter, the officers apologized for any inconveniences caused by the entire imbroglio. Their courtesy after the terrifying experience reminded him of his old high school games' master. School rules prohibited playing soccer in the rain because of lightning. Osaru, along with some of his friends, defied the rules and settled for a good game of soccer in a driving rain. The games master watched the game from his porch. At the conclusion of the game, he marched all the boys to a classroom and lectured them on the danger of lightning and risk of catching a cold. He thereafter proceeded to administer six strokes of the cane and two tablets of aspirin to each culprit. The security officers explained that terrorism was the evil they were trying to prevent. Lunatics with or without causes saw the airport as the best targets for notoriety.

Despite their courtesy, he was shaken and disheveled from the experience, just then, the public-address system called his flight number for boarding.

3

"Welcome to Dallas. It is a warm, sunny day with the temperature at seventy-nine degrees. We hope you have a pleasant stay, and thank you for flying . . ." The voice continued on the aircraft's intercom. The nine-hour flight had seemed more like twenty-four days. He was in a hurry to get to America. America, here he was, but the long flight had diminished his enthusiasm. He just needed some rest.

The airport formalities would have been very brisk but for a little snag. There were two gates, one for American citizens and permanent residents and another for everyone else. The immigration officers spent seconds with each passenger and stamped their passports, and off they vanished behind a wall. It was Osaru's turn. Given his experience at the Lagos airport, he had rehearsed this moment in his mind's eye, providing answers for any contingency. It was not to be.

The immigration officer, a white man in his early thirties with a pencil-thin moustache, asked him only of his expected length of stay, to which he answered, "Three weeks." He wished him a happy stay, or so Osaru thought, as he could barely understand him. The officer appeared to be talking too fast for him to grasp. His passport was stamped, and he was on his way. Clearing customs proved more difficult. He had declared only food items on his customs form. His host, Egbe, a childhood friend, had requested him to bring along a sizeable quantity of *garri* to satisfy his deprived parochial palate.

Garri was the popular staple in his country because of its utility. Originally introduced from the Caribbean, it was produced from cassava tubers. He remembered from childhood from the infrequent visits to his mother's village in the countryside how much effort was put into processing cassava to garri, especially by women. The brown coatings were first peeled off with knives, revealing a sparkling white tuber, which was then ground, fermented, dried, and finally fried in palm oil. The entire process was backbreaking manual labor. Garri consists of tiny grains, almost-powdery, which could be eaten in a variety of ways. Turning it into solid by first pouring it into boiling water was most popular. Eating this with soup remains by far the staple of his people. Now thousands of miles away from home, this local favorite was still the meal of choice for many of his countrymen in diaspora.

The customs officer ripped out the bag of garri and threw it on the floor as if he has been stung by a scorpion. He took it into an inner room for examination. He returned later with a short and stout man with tiny eyeglasses hanging on the bridge of his nose. He could have sworn that the new man was secretly consuming confiscated garri. His biceps looked like those fortified by garri. He had difficulty understanding them. Although their speech was slow, almost slurred, they had a tendency to swallow letters in a word. After several "pardons" and "excuse mes," he gathered that because his garri was wet, it had to be confiscated. He had no problem with that. He had reluctantly brought the sack of garri to please his host. However, there was another problem. The ivory bracelet he was wearing, they explained, was illegal. Osaru would have considered this a joke, but the demeanor of the officers showed otherwise. African elephants were becoming an endangered species due to poaching activities of some unscrupulous hunters. These hunters, he was informed, killed these gentle giants for their ivory tusk, which were then shipped to lucrative markets abroad in Japan, Europe, and America. To prevent the continued decimation of the African elephants, trade in ivory was banned by international agreement.

Osaru was vaguely aware of the issue. He must have heard about the plight of the elephants once or twice before, but he was at a loss to understand how that affected him. In fact, in his country, the elephant problem was a distant blip in their radar of concerns. Elephants were a rare sight in his country, and poaching was virtually unheard of. He learned later that environmentalism and the prevention of cruelty to animals in America were not just sentiments but movements. His immediate problem, however, was that this ivory was a family heirloom. He remembered the solemnity of the occasion his mother had handed it to him. His mother was usually a very quiet and reserved woman, but on this occasion, her calmness and deliberation were exaggerated even for her. She handed it over to him, looked at him squarely in the eyes, and said "This is from your fathers, a trust to you on behalf of your children to come. Take care of it." That was two days before he left Nigeria, which was exactly four days ago. What a trustee he would be to lose a century-old heirloom in four days! He put up his best argument. This was a family heirloom, he explained.

"It has been in my family for ages." He argued that whatever problems plagued the elephants were restricted to the eastern and southern parts of Africa and definitely not West Africa, where poaching, he explained, was virtually nonexistent. In any case, he added, "This heirloom predates the ban." The officers were unconvinced; they insisted that he surrender the bracelet. Parting with the heirloom proved more difficult than he would have thought possible. His immediate reaction was to abandon it since it was standing between him and America. Quite unexpectedly, like a bolt of electricity, his mother's voice, complete with the solemnity and gravity of the occasion he received the heirloom, filtered through his consciousness. He knew now that he could not abandon a family heirloom with laxity. He had to put up a fight in honor of those who had worn it before him. He was sure whoever imposed the ban had good intentions, but they sure could not possibly have intended to outlaw the killing of elephants under any circumstances. What happens to ivory from dead elephants from natural causes? The officers told him politely to take his arguments to Washington, DC, the capital of America. They were merely administrators, not policy makers. Well then, was there an appeal forum? The officers huddled briefly. One of them appeared increasingly very agitated. They retired into an inner room. Meanwhile, the queue behind him was getting longer and restive. What started out as quiet murmurs were now loud rumblings of complaints, indignation, and outright hostility. It appears that passengers all over the world do not like to be kept waiting. The officers emerged with a third officer. The new man was a tall fellow and appeared very relaxed and content. He looked down at Osaru as he was wont with nearly every person and said in a deep baritone, "You say this is family stuff." He nodded his affirmation. "Well, we don't allow stuff like this. Next time you bring stuff like this, you lose it. Okay, pal?" He handed it over to him, and he was free to go. He had won his first victory in America!

4

It had been three days since he arrived. The airport incident was now a distant memory. The practical reality of living in America gradually beginning to wear down his mouth-opening amazement at the splendor and opulence of America. The wide roads, hot showers, constant electricity, fully rugged apartments (even bathroom!), twenty-four-hour television with more channels than he could count, cheap food—the list was endless. His host, Egbe, dotted on him. He was at his beck and call; any and every thing he needed or wanted were provided. He was a perfect host.

Egbe lived in one-bedroom apartment; they called flats apartments in America. It was cozy, clean, and well furnished. Egbe purchased a convertible couch and bed combo prior to his arrival. Osaru slept in the living room because Egbe's girlfriend Pamela (she preferred Pam) practically stayed over every night. They all got along well. Osaru found Egbe's girlfriend, very interesting with, almost with childlike innocence and curiosity. She asked about Africa which revealed a lot of, misconceptions and misinformation. He took his time to reeducate her. No, people did not live on trees, polygamy was weaning, elephants were not household pets, everybody was not starving in Africa. No, Africa was not a country; it was a continent. He came to America on an airplane, not on horseback, people wore clothes in Africa, etc. Discussions with her reminded him of a dialogue he had with a passenger on board his flight from London. The young man was fascinated to know that he was from Africa. He had an African friend. He mentioned a name that Osaru had forgotten and asked if he knew him. Osaru was astonished. How could he know someone just by a first name from an entire continent? Well, he paid back in kind. Later during the flight, he told the young fellow that he had an American friend named John. Did he know him? The nice young man caught the joke, and they laughed over it for a long time.

Pam was receptive and appreciative of the new information he provided. She blamed the school system for her "miseducation." They were a happy trio; the only problem was at night.

Only the bathroom separated the bedroom and the living room. The kitchen, as with in any typical American residence, was attached to the living room. He could never understand this. At home kitchens were tucked away from the view of visitors. On the first night, Osaru had been asleep for some time when he was awakened by a wild scream, then a screech, then a hum, an assortment of incomprehensible words said in repetitive alternating and low tones, almost incantatory. The noise was coming from the bedroom. The cranks from the bed provided a constant refrain for this disjointed, almost-pixilated composition. Having satisfied himself that his hosts were not in any physical danger but actually in blissful physical union, he went back to sleep.

Osaru teased Egbe about the incident the next morning.

"I did not know you have become an iron man lady killer. You had her begging for mercy." Egbe grinned ear to ear and rubbed his chest in parody of his countrymen. He explained that the screams were a calculated hoax, designed to feed his ego.

"You see, women here think or have been led to believe that unless they put on such verbal show during intercourse, the men would feel embarrassed and humiliated at their inability to perform."

"You mean that was fake?"

"You bet, as fake as plastic flowers. They have perfected it to an act. Every girl I have been intimate with here has the same act. You can almost predict the next sigh, shriek, or scream. Honestly, I have told Pam to come off it. I am more secured in my manhood than to be fed this hoax of my virility. She swears it is real, but I know better." Osaru was unconvinced, but if it was staged, she sure was good at it.

On the third day, Pam was off from work and drove him to the driver's license office for a written test. It was still dark when they arrived and joined a fairly long queue. To obtain a driver's license, you had to take both written and practical driving tests. The office did not open until 7:30 a.m., but because they could only test thirty candidates a day, queues formed as early as 5:30 a.m.

The test was administered in batches of fives. You walked right in and took the two-part test, and your results were out ten minutes later. The first part tested your theoretical knowledge of traffic rules while the second tested graphic cognition. Osaru breezed through the tests easily, but the practical examination proved quite formidable. He had been driving since he was seventeen years and did not anticipate any problems. He had been driving with the safety officer on the passenger seat for about three minutes when they approached a traffic light with the green light on, but at about a car length to the light, the green turned to amber. His immediate reaction was to stop, but he remembered that his instruction manual had stated somewhere that if the light was amber and you could not stop immediately, you could proceed, and so he did. The officer turned and looked at him in surprise. Her stern expression told him all was not well. She ordered him back to the office. He had failed his practical test. He could take it again.

His next try two days later was more favorable. He passed but had difficulty with parallel parking. Parallel parking, he later found out, was the Achilles's heels of every new driver. It requires a prospective driver to park a vehicle between two objects by backing into a limited space between them. It essentially tests a driver's skill at parking in limited space without running into other vehicles or the curb. It was simple enough, he thought. In his first two attempts, he almost ran over the curb. On his third try, he squeezed the car in between but at a slant angle. The officer laughed and told him he passed. The beads of sweat on his brow must have elicited her sympathy. After the first two attempts, he had become nervous because rumors had it that failing the test twice automatically disqualified an applicant from taking the test for six months. He now knew enough of America to understand that the ability to drive oneself was as vital as breathing. Six months of relying on others for ingress and egress would be intolerably frustrating.

The Social Security office was filled to standing-room-only capacity. Egbe had set Osaru's agenda the next day after he arrived. Driver's license first, Social Security card, job, bank accounts, etc. A Social Security number, Osaru later learned, was perhaps the most important piece of document in American life. It was required for nearly everything, even death! For a new immigrant, it was a life wire. With a Social Security card, a job was a possibility; without one you were nonexistent in America. However, recent immigration reforms had led to increased difficulties in acquiring one, and even when one was obtained, the document was endorsed "Not Valid for Employment." This endorsement practically made it well nigh impossible to obtain employment. New immigrants had no choice but take what they could get.

After two and a half hours, Osaru finally appeared before an officer standing behind a glass window. Why did he need a Social Security Number during a short vacation in America? she asked. He was prepared. He was on a business trip and needed to open a bank account. What kind of business? she probed further. Fashion and cologne. Any supporting documents?. No. She hesitated but appeared to like him. Well, his card would be in the mail in about two weeks.

With two weeks to wait, Osaru decided it was time to write friends and family. The letters to his sister and mother were easy. Writing Ese was different. He was so choked up with emotion that he could hardly articulate his feelings. He tore off many drafts and eventually went to sleep. He was awakened by a hysterical cry from the bedroom. It was Pam and her frantic scripted (according to Egbe) sexual performance. Tonight, though, it was a bit more maniacal, more urgent, and a lot louder. He was ashamed to admit it; he had caught himself actually looking forward to it, a sort of vicarious sexual gratification. He could almost visualize her tiny body gyrating in consonance with her sound. Her voice had a stereophonic quality to it. In the dark of the night, her insane panting sounded like wailing blues music filtering through the thick walls of a dungeon. He decided to channel his erotic stimulation to writing Ese. This time it came easily.

My darling Ese:

I am writing this at well past midnight. You may be wondering why I have not written earlier. I have been waiting for an opportunity such as this, when ultimate quietness reigns with nothing and nobody to interfere with your pure image in my mind's eye. I look at you now in your full majesty and wonder what makes me deserving of a goddess like you. The answer is nothing but your mercy. That the quivering hands of an unworthy archer can pull cupid's bow and hit a willing and merciful goddess like you must count as one of the wonders of the world. I adore you, my sweet princess, and will always love you.

Love,
Osaru

PS: I am settling down and will inform you of any development. Reply with above address soon.

The noise in the bedroom now was no longer the moaning shrieks of a satisfied lover but had been replaced by sobs, loud bangs, and two angry voices talking above each other. It was getting louder and louder, and he was debating whether it was proper to interfere when Pam bolted out of the bedroom naked with Egbe hot on her heels in pursuit, himself scantily dressed. Osaru handed her the top of his pajamas.

Egbe was boiling over in rage and threatening to do every kind of imaginable harm to her if she did not leave immediately. She stood behind him like a frightened kitten. Osaru was taken aback by this development. He had thought that theirs was a perfectly harmonious relationship. She dotted and drooled all over him, and he was very affectionate with her. The only fault line he could think of was that anytime he brought her up in conversations or commended her, his reaction was rather cool and lukewarm. However, his present state of anger was shocking. They had been friends since he was four and Egbe five. They attended the same elementary and secondary schools, and he never saw his friend go berserk. He knew it would be no use trying to resolve the dispute immediately; tempers were still flaring. He concentrated on separating and calming the warring lovers. He insisted on a temporary cessation of hostilities, at least for the sake of sleeping neighbors.

Egbe agreed on two conditions, that she sleeps in the bedroom alone while he sleeps on the floor in the living room and that she left first thing in the morning. She chose to sleep on the floor in the sitting room.

Osaru woke up the next morning, assuming that Pam was gone. He was walking toward the bedroom when he heard the familiar moaning from the bedroom. They sure made up quicker than he had anticipated. The peace mission he planned for the morning was otiose.

When they were alone, Egbe explained the previous night's incident. Osaru could not contain himself with laughter. According to Egbe, Pam had been complaining that their intimate moments were becoming boring and predictable and suggested spicing it up. She rented X-rated movies and showed Egbe what she required of him. She had nothing new to learn from them. Apparently, Egbe was the cause of the boredom. There was a little problem though; Pam's request that Egbe do things with a part of his body he considered inappropriate. Further, Egbe's marital history was relevant here. His ex-wife, Ophelia, had insisted on his doing the same thing to her before she attended his adjustment-of-status interview with the Immigration and Naturalization Service. Ophelia, according to Egbe, did not shower for two days before she coerced him into performing the act. In a manner of speaking, the oral experience left a sour taste in more ways than one.

Pam's demand therefore touched a raw nerve with Egbe. At first, she requested it only occasionally, but it had of late become impertinent. Last night, he answered her request by saying he was not interested in placing his head in a sewer, or words to that effect. She slapped him on the face. It took him by surprise. She was on target, catching him squarely in the jaw and stunning him. Few sparks flew from his eyes. He least expected her to smack with such ferocity. It threw him into a blind rage, and he was heading for her when she escaped into the relative safety of the living room where Osaru intervened. Well, they made up when she came into the room later. He acquiesced to her request and actually liked it. Osaru's mouth was agape in mock surprise.

His Social Security card arrived on schedule with a mild but significant hyper stance. The "Not Valid for Employment" endorsement was omitted. An immediate employment impediment was removed without effort. The reaction of his friends was indicative of the importance of the omission. His good fortune was well advertised among his folks. The driver's license came in tow. He was ready for the workforce.

His job hunt was aggressive, to say the least. He would set out in the morning, chauffeur driven by Pam, filling out applications at any business that would take them. Pam's knowledge of the city was amazing. She took him to a variety of businesses, restaurants, hotels, temporary agencies, factories, fashion shops, and more. Although he was a certified accountant, Egbe counseled that he stood a better chance of immediate employment if he took the first job available, which by all accounts would be menial.

By weekend it was almost routine; he went in, asked for an application form, filled it, and left with a promise from the clerk of future contact. Three weeks passed with no offer forthcoming. His follow-up calls were politely answered with further promises of future contact. He was getting despondent when Egbe came in one day, grinning. He had good news. A colleague at work had been informed by his immigration lawyer that congress had passed a law granting legal immigrant status to professionals; accountants were included. They were ecstatic. They would visit Egbe's lawyer the next day.

The lawyer's office was tucked away on the ninth floor of a glass tower downtown. The elevator led directly into the office. It was a squeaky-clean place. The secretary was on the phone. When she finally got off, she handed him a consultation form. She was a tall blond woman who apparently was given to sartorial elegance. A middle-aged man who introduced himself as Kirk invited him into an inner office. Kirk, it turned out, was the paralegal. His duty was to conduct a preinterview. Kirk was either a very busy person or was simply untidy. His desk was full of layers of files and sundry papers without symmetry or order to them. Osaru observed that the further he talked, the less interested Kirk seemed. He concluded his notes, collected the consultation fees, and excused himself out of the room. There was absolutely quiet after he left except for classical music, perhaps Mozart, coming from behind Kirk's desk. It made him uncomfortable. He had a feeling that the lawyer may not be of much help. Kirk's demeanor was not very inspiring.

The lawyer introduced himself as Jeffrey Greene but could be called Jeff. His office was clean, lavishly decorated, and scenic. The window blinds were drawn up with the freeway and well-manicured lawns providing the background. Occasionally an airplane would take off or land at a nearby airport. Jeff's desk was a sharp contrast to Kirk's. On the desk were two photo frames, a desk calendar, and a notepad. There were assorted framed certificates on the wall. The furniture looked sophisticated and expensive. Jeff looked every inch a successful lawyer. He dressed the part. After listening to Osaru, he confirmed the existence of a category of professionals' visa, but it was a long and tortuous process. He elaborated further, "You will need a willing employer ready to offer a job. Then there is the labor-certification process through the labor department. They will require you and your potential employer to prove that you are a professional whose skills are of importance to the American economy. The employer must further prove that despite diligent search, they were unable to find a qualified American to fill the position.

"Once labor certification is obtained, it goes for further approval at the state department and finally by the Immigration and Naturalization Service. It is a tedious process but not impossible. The initial step that triggers off the process is finding a willing employer." Jeff's conclusion was an understatement as Osaru, midway through his statement, concluded that the process he was describing was as intricate as a spider's web. Osaru left the law office determined to find a willing employer.

The team of Osaru, Egbe, and Pam spent the evening going through the yellow pages and booking appointments with accounting firms. Two days after his visit to the attorney's office, he was on his way to his first appointment with an accounting firm.

The firm was housed in an old building downtown. The interior was clean, fresh, and elegantly furnished. Coffee smell filled the air. The secretary ushered him to the office of the managing partner a couple of minutes later. He introduced himself as Bill Archer with a strong handshake. Bill, as he preferred to be called, was a strong tall fellow and ensured that everyone knew it. He approached handshakes as arm wrestling contests. He believed firmly that handshakes made impressions, especially first impressions. He had fought in Vietnam, and his office was full of mementos to prove it. He listened intently as Osaru explained his situation. He was sympathetic but apologized profusely for his inability to be of any assistance. His firm could not make the type of commitment he was requesting. He wished him luck.

This pattern was to repeat itself at most of the firms he visited. Some politely declined while others were rude, contemptuous, dismissive, or incredulous for wasting their time. One stood out in his mind because of the bellicosity of the senior partner. He had a premonition that something was amiss when he waited for more than three hours without seeing anybody. Usually, he called days in advance to book an appointment and was promptly attended to. This day was different. There were a lot of comings and goings on in the office while everybody virtually ignored him and his chauffeur and guide, Pam.

By the forth hour, Pam inquired from the receptionist if anything was wrong. There was a meeting, she explained, and Mr. Hoffman had been unexpectedly held over. Could they reschedule for a more convenient day? Pam asked. No, she replied, he might not be disposed to seeing him in the future. This was his only window of opportunity.

After what seemed to be an eternity, a short chubby man emerged. He probably was in his late forties or early fifties but looked worse for the wear. He introduced himself as Dan Hoffman, CPA, owner of Hoffman Chartered Accountants. Osaru restated his story, which was by now worn threadbare.

"You say you are an accountant?" Hoffman asked in apparent disbelief. He had listened quietly with his dark eyes burrowing into Osaru's.

"Yes," he answered.

"Where did you qualify?"

"Nigeria."

"Where is that? In the Caribbean or something?"

"No, Africa"

"They have accountants in Africa!" Hoffman asked Osaru indignantly.

"Yes."

"Well, we deal with real money here, investing people's money, watching people's money, Fortune 500 companies listed on the stock exchange. These are the stuff we deal with. Ever heard of the stock exchange?"

"Yes, I have dealt with companies on the Nigerian stock exchange."

"Nigerian stock exchange! Never heard of it."

"Well, it is the largest in Africa," he replied, slightly irritated by the dismissive tone of Mr. Hoffman.

"Well, I do not think you meet our requirements. Have a good day," he said curtly. "Thanks."

"But, sir, you have not even bothered to review my résumé."

"I did not need to. You do not fit our profile."

The experience was devastating for him. He was slowly coming to the realization that he might be unable to find a willing employer. He must devise and pursue a new strategy. In high school, his favorite line from a popular song was "When one road is closed, another is open." It was time to find another road.

5

It had been eight weeks since he arrived in Dallas, and his energy was once again focused on getting a job, any job. The routine of filing applications in every and all places was getting too monotonous. Pam's enthusiasm was waning. Every now and then, she beg off taking him somewhere because she had a hair appointment or she "wasn't feeling good."

His first mail arrived. It was a thick brown envelope from Nigeria. The stamps had pictures of flying antelopes. He recognized the writing as Ese's. His heart was racing as he ripped open the letter in a huff. She was fine and she hoped he was too. Yes, she was a bit disappointed that he did not write earlier than he did. Life had been slow and colorless without him. Everybody was supportive, but adjusting to life without him was enormously difficult. She was coping as well as she could. Everybody sent their regards and wellwishes. School was still out, and it had been raining heavily. There were rumors of a coup by the military to overthrow the civilian government. Nobody really knew what the situation was as the government was not talking. She had no problem except a minor one. She did not really want to bother him with it, but her sister pressured her to mention it, just in case. Her monthly cycle was about a week and half past due. She is seeing a doctor the following week. Nothing to worry about, but she thought he ought to know. She enclosed a recent photograph of herself and endorsed "Will always love u" at the back. The letter was a jar of honey and vinegar. He was clearly no longer melancholy. His heart glowed with warmth as he read, reread, and analyzed every word and punctuation in the letter. Why did she open with "darling Osaru" and not "my darling Osaru"? And of course, the part about her cycle sank his heart. A baby at this time, to put it mildly, would be an inconvenience. They could not afford one. But it might be a beautiful baby girl just like her mother. Oh! the things he could do with her; play hide and seek, read children's bedside stories to her, throw her up and catch her mid air, watch Disney movies with her, the list of endless things movies showed good dads as did. God! He did not know what to do. Egbe did not help matters. He teased him about fatherhood. She might actually be expecting a set of twins, he said. That would really be trouble. Boy, was he in trouble! They concluded that she might not even be pregnant. Why worry himself to death over a hunch by a girl who knew next to nothing about maternity? Her picture was a source of reassurance and comfort to him. She had her trademark smile, serenity, and tranquility. Her eyes looked blank and questioning, as if asking why he left her. Egbe, the jester, took one look and said he was out of his mind to leave such a girl behind.

"If I were you," he said, "I will not be more than two inches from her at any time."

"That will only smother her," he countered.

"Oh yeah, call it whatever you may. I will be on her like gloves."

"You are right, just as you are on Pam," Osaru replied mordantly.

There had been a giddy, festive atmosphere in the air for some time. It was the tail end of the American football season, and the finals known as Super Bowl was just a week away. As an avid football fan, Osaru was very excited on his first weekend when he learned that there were three football games on television on Sunday. When the game eventually began, he discovered to his chagrin that American football was very different from the kind of football (soccer, as Americans called it) the rest of the world played.

American football was played on turf, artificial or grass, lined with white markers like soccer. However, that was the only similarity. American football was not a complicated game. All a team had to do was have its offense move or advance the oblong ball for at least ten yards on three tries called "downs." If a team failed, it generally kicked or punted the ball to the other team and then attempted to stop the opposing team from making the required yardage. Sounded simple enough except that there were obstacles—formidable obstacles, to be exact. The offensive game revolved around the quarterback, who generally ran and directed the offense. Usually he was the leader of the team. The running back was a vital part of the offense. He ran with the ball, or in football parlance, "carried" the ball. A good offense was one with the double threat of a good quarterback and running back. The offensive squad was complete with receivers, who were usually speedsters of the team, tight end and offensive linemen who were literally giants weighing several tons. The duty of an offensive lineman was to protect the quarterback and running back from the marauding incursions of the opposing team's defensive personnel. Quarterbacks were routinely injured, concussions being the common form of injury. To minimize injuries, players wore pads and protective helmets, but the ferocity of the attacks rendered these protections inadequate. Osaru could not believe the savagery and brutality of the game the first time he watched it. He expected the referees to step in and penalize the offending players for vicious tackles, but nothing happened. In soccer, such tackles could earn a player a life ban. He was clearly disturbed by the violence of the game, but everybody else seemed to accept and enjoy it. With each passing week, the game became more tolerable, and by Super Bowl week, he had chosen a team and was now an average fan of American-style football.

Pam's elder brother, Troy, was an assistant high school football coach and he invited Osaru and Egbe to his Super Bowl party. Troy was a generous and gracious host. He ministered to their every need. He had converted his back room car garage into a sports fortress, complete with a big-screened television to a million sports memorabilia.

There were already five other people in the room when they arrived, some of whom wore red-and-blue jerseys. Beer and popcorn were provided in generous proportions.

Everybody appeared to be in good spirits and having a good time. The level of bellicosity rose with the quantity of beer consumed. Two groups were emerging, each supporting one or the other team. The overwhelming support was for the home team, Dallas Rodeos. The other team was supported by a tiny but fierce, loud, and game group. They argued about the teams' quarterbacks, running backs, previous records, jerseys, hair colors, and more. It made no difference that they could hardly hear each other. In drunken sports arguments, passion, not reason, was the currency of choice. Across the room, seemingly above the fray, Osaru noted a female with strikingly good looks. She appeared to be amused by it all, taking everything in but uttering nothing except polite comments like "That is interesting" and such noncommittal remarks. He concluded that she probably did not like football but had to show up to please her boyfriend, apparently the boy sitting next to her, whipping himself to a feverish pitch. Egbe's voice was by now showing signs of strain. He was a fierce partisan for the home team. Osaru was struck by Egbe's mastery of the game's rules, players, and history. The game was a good one hour away, but television stations were already agog with the pregame shows with analysts (usually football coaches fired for poor performances) trying desperately to earn their pay.

Troy, the ever-affable host, played the fire marshal, dousing arguments that could lead to physical confrontation. Osaru, a sworn teetotaler, was picking a soda from the freezer when he felt someone standing behind him. He turned round and saw her. It was the quiet lady at the end of the couch. She was tall—very tall—elegant, and beautiful. His heart sank and panicked a bit. He stared into her eyes and muttered, "Hello." When she replied, her voice was almost a whisper and hesitant, which hit the ear with a caressing and subtle touch. He recovered soon enough and offered to fetch her a drink. She liked his accent. Where was he from? Pretty soon, they were chatting away. This was a cerebral woman with good looks. He liked her. No, he liked her a lot. No, he loved her!

Go softly now, he warned himself. Ese was his only love. He liked this strange girl, but romance was out of the question.

Denine (her name) moved from her seat to sit with him. They talked about everything except the football game already in progress. The small band of spectators was as much part of the game as the players. They shouted, cheered, or jeered according to their loyalties. Osaru and Denine were engrossed in their conservation; the game was only a background noise. She was a vegetarian and could not understand humans' carnivorous habit. Only when humans understood the relationship between them and other animals and their interconnectedness would man fully appreciate the horrors of his vocation.

Her dad was a history professor and an amateur pilot. Mom was a stage actress but was currently in the Amazon, saving trees in the rainforest.

"Saving trees?" he asked.

"Yes, the rainforest in Brazil is rapidly disappearing because of logging and pressure for farmland. The rainforest is the most valuable source of oxygen for the earth and generally stabilizes its ecosystem. This is very important to mom. She has done this for years."

"Why doesn't she save trees here rather than Brazil?"

"Well, because the devastation there has more ominous consequences for the earth."

"Your mom's concern for the earth's ecosystem is admirable, but developments in the rainforest are driven by economic imperatives. High-minded environmental concerns are possible only after basic economic needs have been met."

"You assume that economic development is irreconcilable with environmental preservation. I beg to differ. Good and sound economic development demands that finite resources be harnessed judiciously."

They bantered back and forth with neither conceding grounds. This was now an ego trip, each trying to stare the other into submission; the contest of ideas was over. By the end of game, they had convinced themselves that they could match each other wit for wit. They exchanged telephone numbers with promises to be in touch.

The game was won by Egbe's team, the Dallas Rodeos, the home team. The entire city was agog with drivers speeding all over town with lights on, horns blaring, and flags flying from the roofs of their vehicles. This was a happy city.

6

Osaru eventually got a job delivering parcels for a fledgling Express Mail company, which was not particularly demanding. It involved collecting parcels from the office and delivering them to addressees, who signed an electronic receipt. He drove a company pickup truck and made an average of seven trips a day. There were many other delivery personnel who hardly knew one another because they were constantly moving in and out. There were no individual offices; a large room served as a rest stop between deliveries.

Delivering parcels to different parts of the metroplex ensured that he met a variety of people. Some boring, others friendly, talkative, or weird. They talked about the weather, and if you were patient, the discussion could vie from astronomy to the latest celebrity scandal. The least appealing aspect of his job was delivering parcels to houses with big dogs. He had never been fond of dogs. In fact he had a crippling fear of dogs. It started when he was a kid, probably at about seven or eight. There was a soccer game between two undefeated youth teams in the local league. His cousins had talked all week about the significance of the game. He was determined to watch it but had to clear two obstacles—obtaining his mother's permission and finding his way unaccompanied to the playground, a first for him. Permission, he reckoned, will not be granted; there was no point seeking. In fact, seeking permission for such a frolic may invite rebuke for harboring and making such an audacious and obnoxious request. The more immediate problem was slipping out of the house unnoticed. His escape plan was working to perfection, and he was surprised at its relative ease. He simply walked through the back door, squeezed between an opening on the back fence, and was free from the prying eyes of his mother and very soon out of sight of curious and inquisitive neighbors. As soon as he was out of his neighborhood and no longer looking over his shoulders to ensure his mother's all-knowing eyes were indeed not on him, he burst into a run. It happened in a flash; he could not remember its exact details, but he was at full speed when he negotiated a corner and ran into a pack of dogs, some big, some mere litters. They deemed his approach an affront on their territorial integrity and charged toward him immediately. His terror was immeasurable. His scream as he fell down at the approach of the dogs must have alarmed the neighbors. He woke up later in a couch with a wet towel wrapped around his head. The surroundings were unfamiliar. He was now fully awake and realized he had to get back home immediately before his mother got wind of it. He tried to get up, but his limbs were uncooperative.

"Rest, my child," a matronly voice said. She was a stranger, but her voice was reassuring. She proceeded to inquire about his parents and their address. He was conscious enough to know that he had to get home as quickly as possible. He summoned all the efforts he could muster and rose to his feet, thanked his host, and made for home. His feet were numbed, but he willed himself home, slipped in unnoticed, and went straight to bed. He was feverish for a couple of days, but his mother, unaware of his midday antics, nursed him back to health. Thereafter, dogs were his mortal enemies. Delivering parcels brought him in frequent contact with his sworn enemies.

It was a cold Monday morning. Mondays were usually the busiest delivery day of the week due to accumulations from the weekend. His second trip took him to the northeastern part of town. It was a bedroom community for the rich, mostly inherited money. They earned their snobbish and standoffish reputation mightily. The supervisors emphasized courtesy on all deliveries but reiterated it when a trip was to "old money," as those neighborhoods were pejoratively referred to. He located the huge mansion tucked away in the middle of dense vegetation and well-tendered lawn.

He pushed the doorbell and waited. After three rings with no response, he walked back to the lawn and looked around the vast compound to satisfy himself that nobody was home. As he walked back to the truck, he thought he heard a noise and instinctively turned; from the corner of his eyes, he saw a huge Asiatic dog racing toward him in blind fury. He was not going to wait to find out its mission. He made his break for the truck. He made it but fumbled the key to the ground, and in that split second, the dog pounced on him. It was a fierce struggle. He was not really a physical specimen. He was slightly built, if not slender. His career in the pugilist science ended early in elementary school after losing all three of his fights. His last fight was particularly memorable. Even now the details and circumstances of the fight remained vivid in his mind's eye. His sister, Ivie, had been ill with malaria fever. On her first day back to school after a week's absence, his mother instructed him to protect her from bullies as she was not physically strong enough to defend herself. At school, a rather-stout boy had threatened to beat her up after school. He kept his promise, and Osaru stepped in to defend her. He put up a spirited effort, but the bully was stronger and quicker. He was the worse for the encounter. He licked his wounds but was proud for defending his sister. He had not fought since.

He was much bigger now, but the dog tore at his calf as he kicked, screamed, and struggled to free himself. This was a very determined dog. It was bent on amputating his limb, albeit without anesthesia. He looked around and spotted a piece of wood (it probably fell off the fence), grabbed it, and in a blind fury, hit the dog on the head. It was a fatal blow. The dog gave one long melancholic growl and lay still with blood gushing out of its nostrils. Just then, an elderly lady walked out of nowhere and ran to the dog, calling, "Zizi, Zizi." She knelt beside it and Osaru. "Poor baby, did he hurt you? Oh, poor baby, oh, poor darling." Realizing that it had no chance of survival, she got up slowly and faced him, visibly shaken. "You should be ashamed of yourself attacking a defenseless dog that viciously."

"Madam, the dog attacked me unprovoked."

"You will pay for this. I am calling the police."

The police station was in a giant concrete building that also housed the county criminal court. There was a foul stench in the air, apparently the body odor of various miscreants who had been denied or shunned a decent shower for days. Two officers reported at the scene of the incident, and he rode in their patrol car to the station. They appeared uninterested in him throughout the ride, only catching glimpses of him occasionally, perhaps, to assure themselves that he had not escaped or was not attempting to.

At the station, he was introduced to another police officer, the desk sergeant, as a suspected burglar. Burglar! He was scandalized. What a transition he had made, from accountant to mail boy and now to burglar. He was well on his way. What next, murderer?

With a steaming cup of coffee on hand, the desk sergeant peered through his reading glasses like an x-ray machine and read him the Miranda warning something to the effect that "you have a right to shut up, but if you decide to talk, whatever you say will be used to nail you!" That was pretty graphic, he thought. He told his story to the sergeant. The sergeant, a man probably in his early fifties, was slow and deliberate, with the mien of having seen it all. He asked Osaru for the telephone number of his employers and left the room. Twenty or so minutes later, he returned.

"Your story checked out, son. You are free to leave. Son, see a doctor immediately. Dog bites can give you rabies."

Egbe counseled him to call an attorney and sue the dog's owner because she ought to have her dog restrained. He had no interest in litigation. Dogs were his mortal enemies. This was merely a continuation of a lifelong war with dogs. He had the upper hand this time. He must be prepared for the next and *ad infinitum.*

7

He called Denine two days after they met at Troy's. She was surprised he did. Guys always promised but never called. They chatted about every topic in the world. She was very inquisitive and yearned to learn more about Africa—the climate, rainforest, bush people, food, dressing habits, and more. It was an exhausting conversation. The semester examination was around the corner, and she was studying at the downtown library daily. Could he join her? He accepted readily. He could use some studies himself as he intended to take an accounting-certification examination later in the year.

He joined her at the library every evening after work. They studied through the evening and walked through the park in the night. He looked forward to the walks. Denine had a fertile mind, capable of elevating the most mundane discussion into a philosophical excursion. She was a veritable fountain of knowledge, a human Wikipedia. Invariably, the arguments drifted to sexism. In her world, men enslaved and kept women down because men were insecure and afraid of women's intelligence. Women have largely overcome these obstacles because of their resilience and emotional stability. The most obvious form of sex discrimination was in Africa, where men married more than one wife!

"Will you allow your wife to marry more than one man?" she asked Osaru.

"Yes, if we were divorced!" Osaru replied, pretending to misunderstand her question.

"Oh, don't be silly. You know what I mean."

"I cannot justify polygamy, but it is important to contextualize it properly and see the practice in its correct historical perceptive. The traditional African society was exclusively agrarian, practicing mainly subsistence farming. There was no agro-technology to speak of. Manpower was the chief resource. It stood to reason that the only avenue for quantitative improvement of production was increased manpower. Polygamy, therefore, was driven by economic imperatives and not a calculated or orchestrated political ploy to oppress women. Polygamy has been waning because of social evolution. As society became progressively less Agrarian, polygamy has become less important and perhaps on its last legs."

"Good riddance! I have never heard a more convoluted argument. Why did same economic imperatives—your words—not result in polyandry? Women could easily have produced as many manpower to sustain the economy such as it was? Obfuscate the issue and grab at straws. You make me sick."

"You make me feverish."

"Oh, come on."

He would get close to her, and their mouths would be locked in a passionate kiss, and then they would go to her apartment.

She had an efficiency apartment on the sixth floor of a downtown complex. It was a tall building of about fifteen floors. Her room was unique for its baldness. Except for books and assorted magazines, it was sparsely furnished. Her family portrait—mom, dad, and Denine—was conspicuously displayed beside a computer monitor. She was not really a great host, but he admired her honesty and lack of pretensions. She knew what she wanted and asked, or perhaps more appropriately, demanded it. She had little or no inhibitions. Her athletic build came in handy, and how he appreciated it. Lying exhausted on the floor (the bed was not strong enough to serve as a *tambori*), they would lie in each other's arm and whisper soft incomprehensible things in each other's ears. At such times, the thought of Ese would jolt him back to reality. In his lonely moments, he was conflicted. Ese was his girl, but his cheating heart lusted for Denine too. She deserved better than a scum like him. She was an angel, and he was not worthy of her, although the "Man cannot live by bread alone" defense was available to him. The story is told of a man whose wife had gone out of state for nursing certification. When she returned eight months later, the babysitter was six months along in the family way, which was not a problem, except that the prospective father was the nurse's husband. Confronted by his irate wife, he retorted, "Man cannot live by bread alone."

Denine was different, an intellectual challenge. He had to maintain a certain level of clarity, coherence, and logic to keep up with her. Her world was vastly different from Ese's. Ese was by no means dense, but she did not wear her intellect around her neck like a sword. She was subtle even when disagreeing, never one to offend, always a conciliator, a troubleshooter, and levelheaded. She was the type of person you wanted your children to grow around. Denine, by contrast, was an intellectual firebrand. She was not one to bite her tongue or suffer fools gladly. Her intellect and knowledge were tools not only for enlightening but squashing all comers who disagreed with her. An argument was a war where all opposing views must not only be repudiated but annihilated. She brought this competitive spirit to every aspect of her life, including sex.

He lay on the carpet after one of their escapades. Her head on his chest, her long braids were beginning to hurt him. So he turned her head slowly around. She looked up, turned herself around, and lay fully on top of him. She was going on a weekend getaway with her dad to Brazil to see her mom. Would he come along? He declined because it was not proper; they were not married.

"Marry me, and propriety is satisfied."

"Do not be silly. Marriage is not something you jump into on a hunch."

"Well, will you marry me?"

"Is that a proposal?" he asked, still in jest.

"Yes," she replied seriously.

"I thought I should be doing that?"

"Says who?"

"Well, it is well and good to be a crusading reformer, but marriage all over the world is a revered institution, with its norms, customs, and usages. I intend to marry once in my lifetime, and I intend to comply with all its traditions."

"Is that a no?" she asked.

"You are very—"

"Is that a no?" she asked again, interrupting him.

"I was just—"

"Is that a no!" She sprang up, moved to the window, pulled the blinds, and stared outside. She was sobbing and trying unsuccessfully to suppress her tears. He had at last peeled off enough of her exterior to discover a soft and venerable yoke. She was now weeping uncontrollably, and he rushed to her, pulled her toward him, and consoled her. He loved her, he said, but marriage was sometime in the future. Marriage was like the peak of a mountain, the apex of a relationship. For now, he was not even sure of his future. For instance, as a non-legal resident with an expired visiting visa, he could not travel out of America. She was quiet for a long time before asking why he had not previously informed her about his status. The occasion did not arise, he explained. How could he regularize his status? she asked. One sure way was marrying a citizen.

He dropped her off at her dad's home halfway across town on Friday afternoon. They were due back on Sunday evening. In the meantime, they resolved to get married on Thursday after her trip. It would be a quiet ceremony; not even her parents would know about it. They would have a more public wedding when they were in better financial stead. Regularizing his status was now her immediate mission, and she handled it with a passion bordering on zealotry. She collected the marriage license from the county office the day after their talk. Before alighting from the car, she kissed him and told him how much she cared for him. She had given him her heart and body and loved him more than words could express, or as she put it, "Linguistic inhibitions to the depth of my emotional feelings." She would rather stay with him than travel, but her mom would be heart-broken. Dad, too, would be lonely in his twin-engine plane without her, his co-pilot. She would miss him and could not wait to see him again soon.

He was still conflicted by the new and unexpected turn in their relationship. Egbe was matter-of-fact about it. The situation, he said, called for cold calculated logic and not sentiments.

"You have to put on your thinking cap," he urged. Yes, Ese was his girl. Yes, she was an angel. Yes, she would be heartbroken. But at the moment, regularizing his stay was top priority. Denine was ready, willing, and able. "Furthermore," he concluded, "you say she is a fantastic lay!" Egbe was his typical self, always jovial but cutting through the chaff with astute observations. He was easily persuaded but was burdened for a while with guilt. He took comfort in the fact that he was at last on the road to regularizing his status. As Egbe put it, "Regularizing your stay is the beginning and end of wisdom." Egbe's argument was sound and reasonable in the circumstance, but he was now emotionally attached to two outstanding women. He had lingering questions to resolve; was he marrying Denine because of his status? If the circumstances were different, would he marry her? The true answer was that he was marrying her because of his status, and if the circumstances were different, he would not be marrying her, at least, not yet. The driving motivation for their impending nuptial was therefore the benefits it wrought. Accordingly, he was a dishonest lowlife, low enough to walk on the belly of a snake. Would she still marry him if she knew this? Maybe he was too harsh on himself. It was true he would not marry her then if he had a choice, but that would be due to his rather-precarious financial situation. He barely earned enough to sustain himself despite his Spartan lifestyle. What about Ese? How would he explain all this to her? What if Denine became pregnant? They had been rather reckless in their escapades, with no protections. That reminded him—Ese had not mentioned anything about her period in her last letter. What if she was really pregnant? By then she would be in her sixth month. How was she coping? He had not even sent her money to take care of herself and the baby if she was indeed pregnant. What a father, husband, and polygamist he was turning out to be!

As he sat in the library, these thoughts raced through his mind. This was his problem—overanalysis. That was why he was often indecisive, or as Egbe put it, "paralysis by analysis." Why could he not be more like Egbe, a happy-go-lucky guy who, if faced with this situation, would take the proverbial "ostrich in the sand" approach. Cross the bridge when you get there, he told himself. That was going to be his approach henceforth. Do what you have to do, and take your lumps as they come. Try as much as he did, the questions persisted. What about Ese? Was this fair to Denine? How did he get himself into this quagmire? In high school, the chaplain always counseled students before examination that their apprehensions were unfounded because the "good Lord never gives us more burden than we can bear." Was he up to this burden?

8

"Amazing grace, how sweet thine sound . . ." In the best of times, this was a sad song. In the present circumstance, it was depressing beyond words. The choir, undeterred, carried on bravely. The caskets were lying at the altar. The minister had the appropriate stern, melancholic look to match the occasion. You could not help but think that he had conducted this type of service too often to be affected by its solemnity. In fact, he looked like the sort of man who could easily move next door immediately to conduct a marriage service with the appropriate demeanor.

Osaru sat in the last row. The program had instructed that no wreaths were allowed; donations could be sent to a named children's hospital instead. He was still in a trance, unable to bring himself to accepting the facts as they were. He had been hoping to wake from a bad dream, but this was the fourth day since his small world fell apart.

It had been another busy Monday at work, and he was quite relieved when he got off. He stopped at the library but could not concentrate. Studying had become almost impossible without Denine, so he went home. The message light on the answering machine was blinking. It was Shannon. He must call immediately she said. Shannon was Denine's closest friend. She had invited Denine to Troy's party. They had known each other since kindergarten school. Denine was the only black girl in class, and Shannon was the only girl who would play with her and not make fun of her hair and skin color. The other girls were particularly cruel with their jokes enriched by stereotypes. A common joke Denine remembered with anger was that her skin was dark because she fell into black mud. Denine remembered going home daily to scrub her skin almost to blisters in a futile attempt to clean the mud. She would cry herself to sleep despite her parents' entreaties. Denine and Shannon had remained inseparable since, and Osaru thought that Shannon was still very protective of her.

He remembered their first meeting as if it were yesterday. They were on their way to dinner when Denine suggested they pick up her friend Shannon. She had not seen her for a week, and she had teased her about the new man in her life.

Shannon was a well-endowed woman, full figured, as she described herself. You really could not say with accuracy that she was fat because her height stood her in good stead. As they say, she carried her weight well. She spoke softly, and you almost had to strain to hear her, but there was something in her voice that made it unforgettable. She probed him from the start, first with her quizzical eyes and later with penetrating questions. She always predicated her questions with "I hope you do not mind my asking" and then moved in to land a deadly uppercut. She must have done this many times. Her deftness and methodical approach was practiced and professional. She got so much out of him that a biographer would only need to add punctuations. Denine watched helplessly, occasionally squeezing his palms gently and serving conspiratorial giggles at funny or awkward moments. When she was done, the two women retreated to the bathroom. Women, he could never understand them. Why did they insist on using the bathroom at the same time? On this occasion, they did not even bother to disguise their inquisition. He was on trial. Shannon's opinion of him would determine the future of his relationship with Denine. Despite all the questions she asked, he knew from experience that decisions such as this were made at an emotional rather than at an intellectual level. It came down to whether she liked him or not. All the questioning was to confirm a conclusion already made at the first handshake. A wise man once said that people did not really think; they merely rearranged their prejudices. That was another thing with women. Why the charade? Why parade him before Shannon? He would never throw Denine or any other woman before his friends for evaluation. Even if they did, he would not be bound by their comments or opinions. In fact, to demonstrate his independence, he may continue a relationship just to prove to them to steer clear of his private affairs.

Women! You never know.

They returned and went about their meals as if nothing had been discussed. When Denine went to the restroom later, Shannon said that she was her baby.

"She is crazy about you. Do not let her into a fool's paradise, please," she pleaded.

"I think the world of her. Is she not gorgeous?" he replied.

Later, Denine told him that Shannon liked him. She thought he was very polished and well-spoken. She was particularly impressed that he opened the doors for them and took his seat after they were seated. He was a gentleman and a "keeper," she had concluded. He accepted the compliments, although he was not quite sure what it all meant.

He had returned Shannon's call, speculating that Denine's travel plans had changed. In a manner of speaking, he was correct; she was never coming back. She was dead. According to Shannon, as soon as Denine and her dad were on international waters off the coast of Florida, they sent a distress signal because of heavy storms and asked for the nearest airport or strip. That was the last time anyone heard of or from them. The coast guard recovered their bodies trapped in the twin-engine plane at the bottom of the ocean near Cuba. Funeral service was set for Thursday. It suddenly was a hot Monday evening.

As he sat at the pew, he still hoped that this was all a mistake. Denine was too alive to be dead. Death was for the old, not the young, healthy, and strong. It was a fairly large group of mourners. The burial was to take place in a cemetery at the outskirts of town. He was surprised to learn that families bought burial plots well in advance. In his superstitious culture, prearranged burial plots were unthinkable. Death was inevitable, but you did not invite it by buying your own grave in advance. Denine's mother could never have imagined at the time of purchase that she would one day be burying her husband and her only child in it at the same time.

It was a cold winter morning with lawns covered in snow and ice. The elements captured the somber mood of the burial party. Blistering wind protested the imminent interment of the bodies. As he stood shivering in the cold, he reflected on the good times they had together—her laughter, passion, and tears, the hop in her steps as she sprang into her father's compound the last time he saw her. How alive she was just a week ago; tears rolled down his cheeks. He remembered the line from John Donne's Poem "Death be not proud." How accurate. Nothing in the present circumstance elicited pride; death's absoluteness, irreversibility, and finality were uninspiring. He kept muttering to himself, "Death, be not proud," and his tears were now a down pour, and the salty taste surprised him. It had been long since he shed tears.

"Earth to earth," the minister said as they lowered the caskets into the graves. There was a sharp cry of anguish; it was Denine's mom. She had been remarkably restrained until now. She had finally broken down. It was over. Her husband and only child were physically gone forever.

Shannon was relatively strong throughout the entire ceremony. She had to. The responsibility for coordinating every aspect of the burial was hers. Denine's mom was too traumatized to be of any help.

That night he could not sleep. Actually, he had been restless all day. He came home after the funeral and went to bed and drew a blanket over his head. Was there anything he could have done to prevent her death? Could he have talked her out of the flight? Shannon had told him that among other reasons, she traveled to discuss him with her mother. She was very excited and looked forward to introducing him to her parents. She particularly was eager to watch him and her mom engage in verbal acrobatics on feminism, environmentalism, and racial politics. Why did he always lose those he loved? His father, his beloved grade school teacher Mrs. Otas, and even Ese was thousands of miles away.

He woke up the next morning with a headache and an empty stomach. He had not eaten in twenty-four hours. Egbe had left him alone to grieve by tiptoeing around the apartment, attracting little or no attention.

Marshall, Denine's mom, invited him through Shannon to visit her two days after the funeral. She was in company of two other women when they arrived. Who soon excused themselves and left. Denine was a chip off the old block—same mannerisms, the quiet storm, even the dimples on the left cheek. She was grateful that her daughter found love before she left. No, she refused to accept the finality of death. Denine was not dead; she could not die. It was a transition to a higher plane. Now she was among the angels. Oh yes! Her baby, who was already an angel on earth, had now joined the angels in heaven. She showed him her baby pictures. She was a lovely baby, she said, smart, compassionate, strong, and independent. He was struck that she hardly mentioned her husband. She would probably return to the rainforest in a couple of weeks but was not quite sure. There was legal stuff to take care of in the interim. Her husband had a will. He left everything to Denine, and she was next of kin to both Denine and her dad. Since she did not survive him and had died interstate (Who could blame her? How many twenty-one-year-olds made wills?), she had instructed the family attorney to sort things out. Routine tasks like closing bank accounts, canceling credit cards, terminating leases, closing social media addresses, and so forth would take about a week. She also had a lot of items to donate to charity. Did he have a favorite charity that could use clothes? Listening to her was painful, but she appeared to be in charge. She was shouldering her tragedy with a defiance Denine would have been proud of.

He saw her every day. The bus route was quite easy. He would stay with her after work and help with odds and ends. They would invariably talk about Denine. One night after they had been talking for several hours, they abruptly stopped as the radio was beaming "Rock of Ages" by Al Green, and instinctively, they sang along. When they finished, they held each other with tears streaming down their checks. She saw him to the door.

"Where is your car?" she asked.

"I do not have one. I use the bus," he replied.

"I see."

At the airport, they hugged, and she kissed him on the cheek.

"You are like the son I never had," she said.

"Thank you," he replied.

"There is something I need to tell you. The autopsy report showed Denine was pregnant. She probably did not know. I am sorry."

The knot in his stomach that had been gradually disappearing in recent days returned with a vengeance. His limbs were getting numbed. He thought he was going to faint. Her flight to Sao Paulo was ready for boarding. She walked away, just like Denine, with the hop and gait to precision.

"I will call you," she yelled above the noise.

Shannon held his hand as they walked away. He was lost in thought and did not notice that Shannon was not driving her regular car. He sat quietly in the car on the ride home, unable to think or speak. Before she left, she asked whether he could drive. He nodded his affirmation. Why? he asked. Could he drive her home? Marshall left the car for him. She wanted him to have it after her departure. He slumped to the ground.

Denine suggested that they go to the movies, but he thought the beach would be ideal for such a hot day. Eventually, they decided to go to the beach after seeing a movie.

They had been swimming for some time, and the sun was setting. The beach, which had been a beehive of activities earlier, was getting deserted. Pretty soon silhouettes would be all you could see. They still clung to each other like high school kids on a first date. The kisses got more passionate and their breathing more hurried and labored. The waves of the ocean swept them off their feet, and soon they were rolling on the floor of the ocean and in front of a white castle. Its pyramid-shaped roofing gave away its Victorian influence. Denine walked in with a familiarity that surprised him. She had been there several times before; it was her resting place, she explained, just a place to collect and gather herself.

"Who owns it?" he asked.

"I do. I bought it two hundred years ago," she replied.

That was odd; she was only twenty-one, but he was too stunned to argue. She snapped her fingers, and two young women walked in—or more accurately, glided in. Their feet appeared to be covered with smoke or snow; he could not tell. They bowed and handed glasses of juice to them and disappeared. The fireplace was burning brightly; except for its apparent weirdness, it otherwise was a comfortable place. Hymns were filtering through from somewhere not easily identifiable. Denine cuddled and wrapped herself around him. There was an unusual glow to her skin and a coldness to her feet he was uncomfortable with. He was about to tell her to put on sweat socks when he felt a sharp pain in his legs. He looked down and was horrified. Denine had no feet; in their place was a fish's tail. He attempted to jump up, but she held him.

"Do not be afraid, honey. To inhabit this world, you have to be part Aquarian. Come with me to this world. You will be my king and I your queen."

"No, I cannot. I didn't know you were not fully human."

"No, I was wholly human, but this is a different world, I want you to come with me. Please do not leave me. Please don't go," she pleaded.

"I have to go. I must go . . ."

Shannon woke him up and told him that he had been screaming in his sleep. His head was heavy.

He was in a hospital bed with drips attached to his left arm. After a prolonged silence, he said to himself, "She should have died hereafter."

9

It had been six months since Denine's death. Life was beginning to return to normal, albeit less colorful. Ese had written sometime earlier. She was fine. More importantly, not in the family way, as they say. She was back to school and missing him. His parcel-delivery job was just enough to pay his bills, which for some strange reasons were growing faster than his earnings. The car from Denine's mom was a big relief. His commute to work and the library was now less tasking as he was more punctual and less fatigued. Denine, however, remained a presence in his consciousness. He would name his daughter, whenever he had one, after her. She deserved that much.

He had a monotonous routine—work in the morning and library in the evening. He had no social life to speak of, except periodic calls to and from Marshall and Shannon and an occasional dinner with Shannon. Egbe did his best to ease his pain, but he was preparing for his final examination and was rarely at home.

The day started like any other one at work. He clocked in on the electronic time clock and went about sorting out mails for delivery. He returned after delivery in the afternoon and chatted with other employees in the large waiting room. The latest gossip, usually who was sleeping with whom, was on. He did not have any close friend at work except perhaps Yolanda, the dispatch clerk, who called him "real brother." She was chatty and extroverted. Generally, it was just another nondescript day as he sat in the waiting room, sipping iced tea when Vicki, the human-resource secretary, walked in and posted some notice on the big board at the back of the room. It must be one of the hundreds of silly notices they posted daily, he thought.

These people posted notices on everything, from "Remember to eat your vegetables" to "nuclear fallout in Russia." Out of boredom, he took a look at the new notice. No! He could not believe the content. It had a terse and innocuous preamble. The company, it explained, had recently been fined by the immigration authorities for hiring aliens without proper work authorization. To forestall a reoccurrence, management directed that "all employees show proof of valid work authorization within two weeks of posting this notice." It went on to solicit cooperation and procedures for speedy compliance. Needless to say that he had no valid work authorization. His luck had finally ran out. In two weeks, he would be out of a job. It was true that his current job barely paid his bills, but sharing some bills with Egbe had kept him afloat. Without a job, he would be destitute and parasitic— two words he could not come to terms with.

For the next couple of days, he wore his dilemma around his neck like a necklace of lead. He spent the evenings filing applications for employment once again. Days were flying by at a furious pace, and he had only three days left. Egbe, while supportive, had hinted subtly that footing their bills alone would be well nigh impossible. They now occupied a two-bedroom apartment, and Egbe worked only part-time since he started graduate school.

He was sitting in the break room, wearing his problem like a mask on his face, when chatty Yolanda took the chair opposite him.

"Real brother, are you ill?" she asked. "You have not been looking right of late."

"Not really," he answered. He was going through a difficult period but could not discuss it at work. Could he call her at home later? Of course he could, she replied.

He got through to her later in the evening after the phone had been answered by three different voices asking the same question: "Want to talk to Yolanda?" She eventually came through sounding sleepy and uninterested. She soon warmed up.

"Real brother, what is the problem?" she asked. He explained his predicament and imminent termination.

"Well, how does one get a work permit?" she asked. Marrying a citizen was one way, he replied. That was a tough one, she said.

However, she could talk to her father, actually her stepfather and the only father she ever had (her mom was dead), about giving him a job at his restaurant. He owned a restaurant on the north side of town. She, too, was quitting to join him in the restaurant in a fortnight.

He looked forward to seeing her in the morning. She was more understanding and thoughtful than he had ever imagined. She was chatty and flippant. Her clothes were permanently undersized, either too short or too tight, while her makeup was extravagant. No wonder nobody around the office, including Osaru, took her seriously. In fact, he had jokingly told her once to stop shopping at Kidman's. Prior to their conversation the previous night, he would have dismissed her as shallow. Now he had a newfound respect for her. Her sartorial taste and mannerisms notwithstanding, she was a well-grounded and considerate individual. His conversation with her the previous night was easy because she stopped short of asking obvious but embarrassing questions. She counseled him like an elder sister and left him feeling that the situation was not as hopeless as he had imagined.

During lunch she informed him that her dad was willing to offer him a job, but he had to attend an interview. Nothing to worry about, she assured, he just wanted to satisfy himself that he was not a no-good drug addict. He had something against drugs. He was a self-made man who loathed loafers, pimps, drug users, and their irks. Earrings and Jheri-curl hair on men were next to murder in his book. She will take him to the restaurant after work and perhaps grab dinner together afterward.

The interview was a love cakewalk. Mr. John D. Washington, III, was a giant of man. He practically filled every space in the room. When he shook your hand, his palm enveloped yours like a blanket. He wore large eyeglasses with black ropes hanging loosely from the frame. His breathing was a little labored. He wore a permanent frown, almost a scowl, on his face. When he smiled, the scowl folded into sedimented layers. He spoke in a surprisingly soft tenor, which was almost embarrassing for a man his size. He relished hard work and loathed laziness, he said. He had worked with Africans and admired their dedication and hoped he would live up to his expectations. By the way, Yolanda thought highly of him.

Rolly's restaurant was located in a tough part of town—the type of neighborhood you warned your children about. Due to vandalism, most of the buildings were boarded up. With the buildings uninhabited due to neglect, drug dealers used them as warehouses. There had been a running battle between landlords—or slum lords, as they were pejoratively referred to—tenants, housing authorities, and law enforcement agencies. It was a circular blame game. The landlords blamed the unsanitary and dilapidated state of the buildings on the unhygienic, criminal, and indifferent dispositions of the tenants. The tenants blamed stingy and greedy landlords whose sole motivation was profit. Law enforcement castigated both parties as irresponsible. Law enforcement was blamed for indifference to poor neighborhoods. While the parties traded accusations back and forth, the buildings deteriorated below habitable conditions, or criminal activities reached unacceptable levels, usually several murders and running gun battles, and tenants were forced to evacuate. In the meantime, drug dealers moved in and carried out a scorched-earth trade policy. To stem drug trafficking, law enforcement boarded up abandoned buildings, but the ingenuity of drug dealers soon exposed the deficiency of the measure. City officials then escalated their offensive by revoking building licenses and demolishing the buildings. Pictures in the evening news showing tractors demolishing buildings with distraught landlords watching helplessly was not exactly good publicity for the local authorities. Public uproar and charges of racism then forced the authorities to lie low for a while, and the drug dealers were back in business. The neighborhood, meanwhile, grew increasingly derelict and dilapidated.

Rolly's was one of the few businesses that remained and maintained a decent environment. The liquor store, which also served as a check-cashing center, was another. At night, especially Friday nights, it was a beehive of drunks, drug addicts, prostitutes, and sundry undesirables. The grocery store, with its iron barricade, overpriced wares, and the beautiful and magnificent funeral parlor rounded up the entire business district.

He was employed as a busboy, which was considered a step-up. Ordinarily, he should have started as a dishwasher, but nepotism had

enabled him to jump the first rug in the ladder of restaurant hier-
archy. The term was new to him, and he hoped it did not include
driving a bus. As it turned out, a busboy was a kind of man Friday,
a handyman to fix everything that might go wrong or needed to
be taken care of. At Rolly's, there were a myriad of problems. Stray
ketchup on the floor, leaking pipes, burned-out bulbs, blocked sink,
wet floor—the list was endless. Mr. Washington was a veritable task-
master who ran a tight shift. Except for a twenty-minute break a day,
Osaru ran, cleaned, waxed, and carried out various assignments for
nine to ten hours daily until Mr. Washington was satisfied that there
was nothing left undone. He returned home late at night, slumped
into the sofa, and sometimes slept through the night in his work
clothes.

He loathed the job. The menial aspects notwithstanding, the
customers were rude and inconsiderate. His coworkers consisted
mostly of high school kids or dropouts whose only interest appeared
to be the latest song on the radio, who was dating whom, or the
next party venue. Yolanda worked the evening shift, and they were
together for a couple of hours a day. She spent most of her time at the
cash register and her dad's office while he was too busy to talk to her,
but they saw each other on Sundays when the restaurant was closed.

He had been employed at Rolly's for three months now. He
deferred his professional examination because he could not afford
the enrollment fees and was too tired to study. He rarely saw Egbe
these days. Although they still lived together, their schedules made
it impossible for them to be home at the same time. Further, Egbe
recently met a girl he apparently was crazy about.

Osaru was yet to meet her, but Egbe held her in high regard.
She was a great and generous girl, he said. She was a nurse at the
central hospital. She was white, to which Osaru quipped, "Jungle
fever." Usually Egbe would have laughed out loud at his attempt at
humor and probably countered with some witticism of his own. Not
this time. He was quiet, and Osaru thought he detected a frown
on his face. He made nothing of it but was struck by the emphasis
he seemed to place on her nursing profession and generosity, which
he thought were gratuitous. Maybe Egbe was having a bad day, he

thought. Everybody had bad days in this pressure cooker called America. He recalled his hypothesis about the differences in work attitudes between Nigeria and America, to the effect that In America, life was incidental to work, while in Nigeria, work was incidental to life. Perhaps development had its price; he was uncertain if the trade-off was worth it.

It was Sunday evening; he was out with Yolanda—movies, restaurant, and then movies again. If it were left to him, he would rather have stayed home to rest, but she insisted. She was his bene-factor, and he felt a sense of obligation. He was very respectful of her physical integrity—almost deferential. She was just his friend, and he would not dare abuse her generosity. At the movies, the first time they went out, she chatted away as was her wont and at times held his hands and nothing more.

They were back at the movies after dinner. She wanted to see a new movie starring a group of young black women forced into robbery by economic hardship. The movie had its usual mindless bloodletting and car crashes but succeeded in vividly capturing the plight of the underclass. During a particularly moving scene, Yolanda shifted closer to him and held him tightly; he reciprocated by gently stroking her braided hair. He felt her hand down the recess of his pants, and a surge of excitement went through him. They kissed. It was long and passionate. She was rather adept at this. Oh, the things she could do with her tongue! As abruptly as they had started, she pulled back and asked, "What do you think I am?" He was taken aback. What did she mean? He did not initiate this. What was an appropriate answer in the circumstance? The cardinal rule was when in doubt, flatter.

"The greatest girl on earth," he replied.

"Why have you never said that before?"

"I did not want you to think I was taking advantage of you or—"

"Take advantage of me. Let's go."

He was lying exhausted on the couch when Egbe and a lady walked in. He had just seen Yolanda off; she had a hair appointment. Their amorous adventure was a new experience for him. He had been at the depth of collapse but wanted every moment of it, a feeling that was sort of "Stop it. I like it." Egbe introduced his companion as Linda. She was short and thickset, certainly not Egbe's usual type. They engaged in polite conversation. Egbe had told her so much about him and hoped he liked living in America. She invited him to stop by when he could for dinner someday at her house. He really was not in the mood for an extensive conversation. He politely made his excuse and promptly went to sleep.

The professional basketball league's postseason was on. With a galaxy of stars on display, it was a big television draw. That Sunday afternoon, three games were scheduled to air consecutively. Osaru and Egbe, for the first time in months, were spending the entire day together at home.

Their relationship was strained, if not frosty. Osaru attributed this to their tight schedules but was disturbed because Egbe was a comedian who could get a laugh from a funeral procession. His self-deprecating humor had always made him easy to get along with. His recent withdrawn and long face was uncharacteristic. Osaru resolved to probe his friend's source of anguish. Egbe, who was usually boisterous and loquacious during ball games, was taciturn on this occasion. His answers to all inquiries were short and sometimes sarcastic. Osaru persisted with an obduracy that finally pierced Egbe's defenses. Yes, he was ticked off by a telephone conversation they had a couple of weeks earlier wherein Osaru had made disparaging remarks about Linda, his girlfriend. The comments were inappropriate, inexcusable, and unacceptable, he said. Osaru had no right to disrespect his girlfriend. He had observed his contemptuous and condescending attitude toward her the day he introduced them. Not everybody could have girlfriends who were centerfold materials, he concluded angrily. Osaru was stunned by his friend's tirade. They had both engaged in locker-room humor for years. It was mainly harmless vulgar jokes. In grade school, they were the youngest and smallest in their class. The girls were much bigger and treated them like younger siblings. They liked the attention but were frustrated by the constant rebuff of their amorous advances, such as it were. They got even by saying the most disparaging things about the girls, albeit behind their backs. In high school, their situation with women was not much different. They attended an all-boys high school. The nearest girls' high school was about twenty miles away. The opportunities for meeting girls were few and far between. Annual interhouse sports competitions provided such rare avenues. Schools in the district usually organized intraschool athletic competitions annually, with teams representing various halls of residence, commonly called "house" and named after some prominent politician or founding principal. Students from other schools in the district were invited, and their relay teams competed against one another.

One interhouse sports which remained a patch of green in his garden of memories was held in his fourth year of high school. He remembered it vividly as if it were yesterday. He met Ese on that occasion.

The entire student population worked hard all week cleaning the large school compound. All routes into the school were lined with whitewashed stones, with well-manicured lawns and flowers providing the background. The sports arena was properly marked with white paint and provided perfect postcard view against a lush green background. Seats were provided on one side of the field inside hired brightly colored canopies, with the names of their owners conspicuously displayed, one progressive union or the other.

Students were woken up at 5.00 a.m., an hour earlier than usual, to put finishing touches to preparations. Unpaved roads were watered, swept, and raked to give them long spiral linings. Competition was scheduled to kickoff at 4:00 p.m., but by 11:00 a.m., the crowd was already gathering. Their high school attracted more spectators than others because it had won the state's athletic championships for three consecutive years.

Osaru and Egbe were members of the same house, and Egbe was taking part in the "march past." March past was simply the presentation of colors while filing past the crowd and invited dignitaries. Precision marching was emphasized and scored like other events. Against the background of marshal music provided by the local police band and a plethora of colors, a gait and joyous mood was set for the day. Osaru was a good athlete and competed in three events, the maximum allowable. He had only one for the day, the other finals having been concluded a day prior to the main event. His event, the long jump, had an early billing. He came in second and secured valuable points for his team. It was time to roam around in his track suit with a medal dangling conspicuously around his neck to talk to any girl willing to listen. He found Egbe, and they started "circulating," as they put it. This was not an exact science; it, however, required tact and the ability to accept rejection without the loss of self-esteem or suffer diffidence. They would spot a girl from the corner of their eyes, decide on who was to take her on, and more often than not returned to a designated spot after another rejection.

The toughest girls were those who hung out in pairs or more. They would not only turn them down but also complete the humiliation with conspiratorial giggles. Osaru resented their giggling more than anything else. What were they giggling about anyway? Didn't a wise man once say that laughter was the symptom of an empty mind.

The day was far spent, and their luck was running out. This was a critical year for them to secure a girlfriend because it was their fourth. In the first three years of high school, belonging to the "boys' club" (that is, you had no girlfriend) was excusable and accepted. Youth and innocence were good-enough folders against the scorns and sneers of peers. In the fourth and fifth years, membership in the boys' club was inexcusable and the height of social backwardness, or in school parlance, "lacking," complete with all its pejorative connotations. They retreated to their observatory and voiced their frustrations by calling the girls all kinds of vituperative epithets they knew. They now understood the state of mind that spurned the Isaki lore. School legend had it that Isaki, then in the fifth and final year of high school, was "lacking." At his last interhouse sports competition, having failed to impress any girl, he finally stuck to one and in desperation said, "I have ten shirts and five trousers and four pairs of shoes." As they say, a tale retold is a tale altered. Accordingly, this legend has several versions, some rather extravagant and colorful. Needless to say that it was a legend worn threadbare by repetition and the source of many fist-cuffs. Nothing invited more scorn, ridicule, and laughter over being called a "lacking Isaki."

The highlight of the day's competitions was the four-by-one-hundred-meter relay for senior boys. The participants were usually boys in their fourth and fifth years. Two of the participants that year were national champions in the short distances. Final preparations for the race was on when there was a sudden twist in the weather. The sun vanished and the sky darkened almost immediately and, within a twinkle of an eye, let out a fierce torrential rain typical of the tropics. The crowd scattered, seeking refuge in the nearest set of buildings.

Osaru scrambled to a classroom nearby. As he stood in a corner of the room, smartering from the rather-disappointing day, he observed from the corner of his eyes a girl trying desperately to keep dry. Apparently, she was unable to escape in time to avoid the rain. The wind blew some rain into the room through broken windows, and she was taking the brunt of it as her pinafore dress provided inadequate protection. He walked to her and offered his track's windbreaker; she smiled and graciously accepted. He was smitten by her electrifying smile which revealed perfect dentition. They struck a conversation. She thought he was too young to be in the fourth year of high school, and he thought she was too beautiful to be tormented by rain. He used his tiny body to shield her. By the time the rain relented, they had exchanged addresses with promises to write. Her school bus was blaring its horn; it was time for her to leave. She kissed him on the cheek ever so gently and was gone. He could not believe his good fortune; he had to find Egbe. He located him later in the hostel, and Egbe demanded that he relate the encounter in "slow motion." He told his tale with relish and embellishment and concluded with the satisfactory exhilaration of a conqueror. He was no longer "lacking"! His membership in the boys' club was automatically terminated. The next step was composing a love letter. They resolved to seek the advice and help of experienced senior boys in their new endeavor. Written communication was actually the bulk of teenage relationship. They hardly saw the girls anyway, except during vacations. The act of letter writing was therefore crucial to the survival and sustenance of a relationship. It required a delicate balancing of expression of deep emotion without going overboard. A letter could be intercepted by school authorities, and you wanted to write a letter that would not be too embarrassing if read in public. The boy with the gift of composition and eloquence was king, and all lovestruck youngsters beat the bush to his throne.

Osaru had found his Juliet and letter writing was not going to impede his cupid's arrow. His new love's name was Ese.

So they plotted strategies for attracting women, shared their modest successes and humiliating failures together since grade school, and never disagreed once in that regard. This was new territory. He tried to explain to Egbe that he was tired the day he met Linda. In any case, he was sure Egbe was not serious, Linda was not his type of girl; Pam was more like it, but if he was serious, he wished him luck.

Egbe, visibly angry, replied, "It is the same arrogance I cannot stand. Who are you to tell me who is or is not my type? That has always been your problem, arrogance, being a know-it-all, what is good and bad for everybody. I am sorry. I will not be bullied by you any longer. I am my own man! And the earlier you learn that, the better!" The vehemence of his tirade left Osaru stunned and speechless.

10

According to his mother, he was born on a raining night in April. The joke was that he was in such a hurry that he was delivered in the back seat of a taxi cab on the way to the hospital. He was the first child of a young couple who were excited at starting a family. Their excitement was tempered when his father lost his job with the local railway company two weeks after his birth. His father, although dejected, shrugged off his dismissal with religious stoicism, saying, "The Lord had blessed me. Who am I to complain?" On the twenty-first day after his birth, he was given his name, Osarumwense, Osaru for short, meaning "The Lord has done good by me." He had grown into a healthy, active, and quizzical little boy. His curiosity and importunate questions earned him the nickname Parrot.

Two years later, his parents had another child, a girl named Ivie, meaning "precious." She was the most beautiful girl in the world. He loved and doted on her from day one.

A year after his sister's birth, his serene world was suddenly invaded by a group of elders speaking in frantic low tones. There was something wrong, but he could not tell what. He ran to his mother for explanation, only to find her sobbing and surrounded by other women, some of whom were familiar visitors to the house. He held her and began to cry too. Later in the evening, a group of young men took a long wooden box into his father's bedroom; it was his father's corpse. He had not come home last night. His mother explained to him that he was working late. His body was discovered dangling on a rope tied to a pole in a nearby school yard. His suicide note stated that he could longer provide for his young family. He preferred death to the humiliation of failure. To his family, he expressed his eternal regrets. Later his mother explained to him that his father had joined the angels. That was not bad, he thought.

"When will he come back?" he asked.

"Never," she replied, looking away to hide her tears.

A couple of days later, there was an all-night party where he was the center of attention. He liked it. If joining the angels always involved this kind of party, then he was all for it, although never coming back aspect was worrisome. On the fourth day, his father's body was interred, and for the first time, he saw his motionless body and shouted, "Look at Daddy!" Why was he still there and not with the angels? He would ask his mother later, he resolved.

One morning his mother woke him up earlier than usual. He was going to school for the first time. The school was close by. Every child in the neighborhood had attended it for ages. At school, a frail-looking man and his mother were engaged in a spirited argument. He instinctively disliked the man. He could not be admitted, he said, because he was underaged and not ready for school. He was ready, his mother had insisted. The man asked Osaru to place his right hand across the top of his head and touch the top of his left ear. His hand was too short to make the distance. The experiment conclusively disqualified him from admission, the man said. No, his mother argued, he was ready; his height notwithstanding, he was intelligent enough to cope with school. They went back and forth for a while until a lady walked in and greeted his mother with some familiarity. After they both restated their positions to her, she asked to speak to the man alone. When they returned, the man apologized and said he could begin school immediately. Later he would learn that the frail man was the headmaster or principal, and the good lady, his deputy. Apparently, she had informed him that the little boy had recently lost his father, and his mother needed to get out of the house to provide for the family while school served as day care for him. Thus began his school career.

His first day of school was remarkable for its ordinariness. He put on his new school uniform (a navy-blue cotton shirt and shorts) and ran beside the big boy next door his mother had handed him to.

In class, he hardly understood any of the sounds the children repeated after the teacher countless times. The teacher would shout a number or a letter, and the class would chorus it after her. Occasionally, the class was distracted by an argument or a fight among the pupils, and the teacher, a middle-aged female, would quell the disturbance and immediately break into a song, and the class will follow suit.

During breaks he observed that all the other children were bigger and approached one another with a familiarity suggestive of long acquaintance. None of the kids talked to him, so he withdrew into himself. This feeling had remained with him all his life, the feeling that everybody else was up to something to which he was excluded. Although he enjoyed the classes, break periods were long and lonely. School was not all the fun he had imagined. He could not wait to run home and tell his mother that he was not going back.

After school, he ran home as fast as his legs could carry him, but the doors were locked, and his persistent knocks went unanswered. Madam Owie called out his name; she was her mother's friend from the next compound. She would take care of him until his mother's return from her stall in the market in the evening, she said.

He anxiously awaited her return. When she did, he hugged her excitedly and clung tightly to her. He had never been separated from her before that day, and it was the longest they had been apart in his young life. He related his experience in school to her, and she appeared pleased until he announced he was not going back. She was apparently taken aback and stated emphatically after a long pause that he was going back because that is what his father "would have wanted." That was a mantra she would invoke over and over again in his life.

On his third day at school, he was picking up a duster to wipe his slate when he accidentally bumped into the big writing board in front of the class. The board, which stood on a three-legged high stool, wobbled unsteadily and crashed on the floor. The classroom was a large hall with only a quarter of the space occupied by the pupils. The sound of the fall echoing in the large hall was deafening. The teacher, who was temporarily out of the class, rushed in with another male teacher in tow. The frightened pupils retreated to the far recesses of the room, shrieking and calling for their parents.

He was taken to the teacher's room and repeatedly whacked on the buttocks. He returned to class in tears and resolved never to return to school. He was still sobbing during break when a little boy tapped him on the shoulder and began consoling him. His name was Egbe, and they had been friends since.

He now truly resented school. It took threats and gift incentives to get him ready for school each morning. One Sunday afternoon, Uncle Jaja, his father's younger brother, came visiting and informed him that he would be living with him henceforth but would remain in his old school. Uncle Jaja had recently married and worked for the local television station.

He lived with Uncle Jaja for six months and resented every minute of it. His uncle's wife, Aunt Maria, who insisted on being called "sister," treated him like an adult. He was only four, but she expected him to perform chores in the house, and failure was visited with admonition or corporal punishment, depending on her whims. He longed for his mother, whom he saw occasionally now. His sister, who had turned two, was beginning to talk the last time he saw her. How he wished they all could be together again. He was too scared of his uncle to ask about leaving. His opportunity came in the form of a near disaster. His uncle's wife had instructed him to wash some dishes after dinner. He fell asleep and forgot. In the morning, she became irate and went into a fit of anger. His punishment was forfeiture of breakfast. During a break at school, he was walking out of the classroom when he slumped to the floor and passed out.

He woke up later in the headmaster's office with the school dispenser at his side. After a few questions, she determined that hunger and not a serious medical condition was the problem. He was fed and kept in the office until the close of school.

At home in the evening, his mother rushed in, and after angry verbal exchanges with his uncle and his wife, she grabbed him by the hand, and they marched towards home and freedom. As they walked through the deserted footpath, he could hear her crying and felt a sense of guilt for her troubles. He promised himself never to make her cry again. He would be a good boy so that she did not send him away again to the wicked aunt.

"Mama, I am sorry," he said.

"Osaru, it is not your fault. I should not have sent you away."

"Mama, I will not leave you again."

"No! I will not let you go ever again!" It was very dark, and only their footsteps disturbed the unending screech of insects.

After that his life had been fairly normal and filled with happy memories. In the third grade, he began to really enjoy school because the teacher, Mrs. Otas, took a special interest in him. She made him class monitor (leader), a position hitherto reserved for the biggest boy in class. School was also beginning to have structure and purpose for him and not just a place you went until your mother returned in the evening. His grades were dramatically up and near the top of the class. His younger sister had now joined him in school.

At the end of the school year, Mrs. Otas told him that she was taking some time off to have a baby. He observed that her stomach was expanding by the day and concluded that she must be having too much to eat. After all, she was a teacher and therefore had a lot of money!

He had often wondered what teachers ate and concluded it must definitely be something other than what ordinary folks like himself ate. Did teachers use the bathroom? Absolutely not! How dare he harbor such mundane thoughts about teachers!

When school resumed, Mrs. Otas did not return. The headmaster announced one day during morning devotion that she was dead. She had died during childbirth. His mother did her best to console him. No, she was not dead, she said; she had merely joined the angels. Why did people he loved always join the angels?

"Why don't they take other people?" he asked.

"They do," she assured him. "You just don't know about them."

In the final year of grade school, evening classes were mandatory for extra preparations for the high school entrance examination. A fee was required. On the third evening of classes, a list of fee defaulters was read with instructions to pay the following day or stop attendance. His mother explained to him that the fee was unaffordable. He withdrew and studied at home instead. He passed and was admitted to two schools. One was the oldest and most prestigious high school in the state, but the fee was prohibitive and out of his mother's reach. So he settled for the community high school at the outskirts of town, which had offered him a tuition scholarship. Boarding was, however, mandatory. The choice was made more palatable because Egbe would be attending the same school.

High school was blissful for the most part. It was the first time he was leaving home and the protective cocoon of his mother. She told him to be a man.

"Men do not cry," she said as she prepared to leave the school dormitory. "Study hard and obey your teachers."

In the first two years, he was a mediocre student, which was a true reflection of his efforts. An incident during vacation at the end of the second year changed his attitude. He had been home for about a week for Christmas holidays when two women came to the house to see his mother.

They, unlike the usual friendly visitors, were stern and businesslike. His mother had not returned from her stall at the market, but they took their seats on the long bench in the patio. He went about his business and promptly forgot about them. Moments later he heard raised voices including his mother's and ran out. She was in a heated argument with the women until neighbors intervened. They left with a promise to come back soon. His sister explained to him the source of the fracas. Their mother borrowed some money from a credit union to pay his boarding fees at compound interest. She had defaulted on two scheduled payments because fire gutted her wares at the market warehouse some months earlier. The two women were professional collectors notorious for their ruthless efficiency. After that, he resolved to study hard to earn enough money to repay her debt and take care of her.

He, in fact, became a very good student and, at the end of his final year in high school, won two scholarships to study accounting at the local university and the Federal University in Lagos. Egbe did not fare as well and left for America during the summer. While in college, he took a part-time job at the library to supplement the family income because his sister, Ivie, was now in high school, and the strain on his mother had grown considerably heavier.

He sat still in the couch, looking at Egbe, too shocked to respond to his charges of arrogance as different incidents in his life flashed through his mind. Arrogance! Unbelievable. How could he be arrogant? How dare he be arrogant? That was one vice he was incapable of. He had been dealt such an unfair hand in life that arrogance was a word he could not identify with. He knew who he was and whence he came from. If anyone else had made that accusation, he would have dismissed it as an ignorant ranting, but coming from Egbe, his lifelong friend, who knew him like the back of his palm through his trials and tribulations, rendered him speechless. This was Egbe, who had everything—father, mother, brothers, sisters—the same Egbe whose closet's old clothes, shoes, and toys he salvaged. He shook his head and walked out.

11

Egbe had always resented Osaru's arrogance. It was true he had everything, a dad and mom, while Osaru lost his dad early. However, he had always felt that everybody, including the teachers and virtually every adult, overcompensated for his loss in various forms of preferential treatment. In time, he felt Osaru expected to be treated differently, albeit better than others. In school, he was bright, but teachers fell over themselves to shower him with favors. Girls preferred Osaru to him, even when Osaru wore rejects from his wardrobe. Yes, he resented his friend, not out of jealousy but for his arrogance and sense of entitlement.

One day Egbe informed Osaru that their lease was expiring at the month's end and that he was moving in with Linda. Osaru was devastated; quite apart from losing his friend, he could not afford an apartment on his own. He had been able to keep the grass below his feet so far because they shared expenses. Yolanda, with her ultra-sensitive antennae, ferreted his problems out of him at work and, as was now her wont, provided an immediate solution. She had been toying with the idea of moving out of home for some time, but her father would not hear it. They could move in together. Although Mr. Washington liked him, he may not approve because they would be "living in sin." He got the hint.

Later that evening, he called her and proposed marriage.

"Must I answer right away?"

"You don't have to, but I will—"

"Shhhh, yes! I will, I will!" she screamed, obviously excited. He should have been too but was not. Was he marrying her for the right reasons? Was he getting married because he needed a roommate? What about Ese? Was he casually ending a relationship without the courtesy of informing her? Was Yolanda the right girl for him? These questions tormented him, but he knew he had to proceed with the marriage regardless, and that saddened him.

Mr. Washington was delighted. In an unusual show of emotion, he hugged Osaru and called him *son*. He had worked hard all his life and had been worried that his business would fall into ruins on his demise, but now there was a son to carry on after him.

Their marriage was elaborate and made the pages of the community newspaper that anyone hardly read. The publisher usually dumped scores of the paper on Fridays at the doorstep of every local business while clearing the last batch. In the community, reading was a lost art, gone the way of the dinosaurs.

With Mr. Washington's assistance, they moved into a home. Meanwhile, he became *de facto* manager of the restaurant. There was now routine and normalcy in his life. Yolanda technically still worked at the restaurant, but her assignment was limited to purchasing supplies. He was happy for the first time in a long while. It was time to regularize his stay.

The immigration lawyer came highly recommended. He had worked with the immigration service for well over a decade. Word on the street was that he still had an inside track because his wife worked for the service. Veterans of immigration battles in his community showed him their scars and spoke of the attorney with pontifical reverence. But for him, they said, they would have long been deported or removed from the US. If John Underhill could not regularize your stay, nobody could.

Osaru and Yolanda walked into Mr. Underhill's office with great expectations. They were disappointed. For starters, his office was sparsely furnished. The furniture was old and unkempt. The phone screeched incessantly. The air was heavy and stale with coffee smell. Mr. Underhill was a short man with a bald head. He was fighting his baldness bravely. He slicked the two or three strands of hair still hanging on top of his head from one ear to the other. He wore eyeglasses that almost matched the circumference of his eyes balls on the bridge of his nose. He peered at you from the top of the glasses and gave the impression that he used them as x-ray equipment. In general, he was a severe-looking man.

He spoke in a soothing, unhurried tone. Osaru figured out right away why he was an effective attorney; he seduced with his voice. It was reassuring and convincing and left no doubt that he knew of what he spoke. He was meticulous and could elicit answers from you without appearing to do so. The questions were camouflaged inside a discussion on another topic. He could be discussing his last "safari" and how much fun it had been and then without warning casually slip in a question about how Osaru met Yolanda. By the time they left, he had questioned them on everything about themselves, from how they met, the length of their courtship, the number and color of their household appliances, their pets, their favorite drink, their meals, music, flowers, movies, and more. It was a virtuoso performance. They were impressed.

He gave them a bundle of forms and a list of items required for processing. They promised to return the forms within a week and pay part of the attorney's fee. He was a considerate lawyer, he said; he never insisted on full payment of his fees up front. He understood the teething financial problems of new immigrants. He catered to their needs by working out a tolerable payment plan. All he asked was that the plan be scrupulously adhered to.

It had been four days since they visited the attorney's office and were scheduled to visit again the following day, but a secretary from his office called to cancel. Mr. Underhill was going out of town for a friend's funeral; they rescheduled for Wednesday the following week because that was Yolanda's hair day. She would go to the salon as soon as they were through with the attorney. Her hair used to look great until she started coloring it; now it was difficult to tell what it was after it had gone through all the shades of the rainbow. Osaru was perplexed by her obsession with her hair but had learned early not to be too free with his observations. Experience had taught him that complimenting her hairstyle was prudent no matter how repulsive it actually was to him. Several scowls, rebuffs, and smacks later, he was now adept at gratuitous compliments. Initially the charade galled him, but it was not worth going to war over. When you are married long enough, you pick your battles. After all, it was her hair!

On Wednesday they canceled their appointment with the attorney; Yolanda had come down with a nasty cold the previous night which did not improve by morning. She assured him that she would be fine; she just needed some rest and over-the-counter medication. At work he called every hour, and she sounded better as the day progressed. It was about four in the afternoon; the lunch-hour rush was over, and dinner was about an hour and a half away. There usually was a lull in activities at the restaurant during that period. Osaru called Yolanda for what he hoped would be an extended conversation about odds and ends. The phone rang continuously unanswered. He hung up and dialed again without response. He was worried now; perhaps she slept off, went to the store, or was taking a shower. He tried again after five minutes with the same result. After several futile attempts, he informed Mr. Washington of his apprehensions and dashed home. She was home, teary-eyed, shivering and curled in a fetal position. He was alarmed. She refused to respond to any of his questions. He got closer to her and attempted to turn her over to hold her, but she pushed him away and muttered, "You lied to me, you lied to me. Tell me it ain't true." She sprang up, smacked him in the chest, and screamed, "Tell me it ain't true." She kept repeating it. He could not understand the source of her anguish, but she kept crying and repeating her lines. There was no doubt that she was in deep pain, and that he was the source of that pain was also obvious. The only missing link was how he managed that feat without being aware or present at the scene of the crime! After many unsuccessful entreaties to squeeze the story out of her, he called her father. At first, she would not talk to him either, so he put him on the speakerphone, and his reassuring voice and her favorite nickname, Pucky, finally induced a response. She gushed it out in hurting staccato.

"Daddy, he is married in Nigeria. His wife wrote from his country!" His wife? What wife and what letter? he asked. She pointed to the mirror dresser. The unmistakable sky-blue envelope with the picture of a leopard in motion on the stamp sat there. He glanced through it, and there it was: "your wife, Ese." He was paralyzed and speechless.

The letter was short, accusatory, restrained, and sweet at the same time. Ese, the ever-considerate Ese, was controlled even in her anger. Why did he abandon her? Why had he not written or replied to all her letters? Could he imagine the heartaches and sleepless nights he had caused and continue to caused her? Did he know the amount of ridicule and sniveling remarks she was putting up with on his account? Did he understand the humiliation and embarrassment of attending countless weddings of her friends? The endless questions and pleading of her mother? The threats from her father? She had endured all because of her love for and belief in him. She knew he was a man of honor and, in the end, would fulfill his commitment to marry her. Did he not always say that they were already married and that ceremonies were merely cosmetic rituals. However, his prolonged silence was beginning to erode her resolve and question her own sanity. If she had unwittingly incurred his wrath, she sought his forgiveness. By the way, she only recently secured his current address from Egbe, when he was home on vacation.

Actually, that was the first question he was pondering. It made sense now. Egbe was the culprit. He had not seen or heard from his friend in six months, and this was his way of settling whatever scores there were. His anger was rising, but he knew he had bigger problems at hand. His people say that only a fool hunts for crickets with his toenails when the carcass of an elephant is at his disposal.

The letter, he argued, was exculpatory. Yes, she was his girlfriend in Nigeria. Of course, she should have known that he was not a monk before they met. He was sure she, too, must have had serious relationships that fizzled out in the past. The letter itself showed there was no communication between them. He had moved on with his life; if she chose to hold on to the past, that was unfortunate, but there was nothing he could do about it. He might as well have been talking to a stone; she completely ignored him. He went on and on like a man possessed, begging to be spared the executioner's axe. He called her father and explained the situation, and he promised to help.

For the next couple of days, the atmosphere in their home was tense. She snapped at the slightest provocation and insisted that he sleep in the couch in the living room. He spent longer hours at the restaurant and gingerly walked his way around the house in the few hours he was there. Yolanda refused to leave home. She was mourning, she said, the death of the only love she ever knew. He was dead as far she was concerned.

Mr. Washington put in a lot of effort to arrange a truce but was getting frustrated by his failure. One day he called him to his office and expressed his frustration. The stumbling block, he said, was that someone had convinced her that their marriage was pretextual to enable him to regularize his stay in the country. The fact that they went to an attorney in that regard the previous week made any argument to the contrary implausible to her.

It was on a cold November night two weeks later that she abruptly ended hostilities and arranged peace on her terms. He was sleeping in the couch, where he had been banished, when he felt something on his head. He did not think too much of it. The couch was relatively small for him; he had to curl into a ball to fit in. Nudging his body against the rather-hard leather couch was a nightly rite of passage. This time it was different. The methodical rhythm of a warm feminine hand was unmistakable. The gentle sobs were at first a distant echo but grew persistent and louder and louder. He opened his eyes; it was Yolanda.

"Baby, I am sorry," he said.

"I am sorry too," she replied. Relations were normalized. She would forgive him, but he must demonstrate that their marriage was not a sham. Until she was convinced otherwise, there would be a freeze on his regularization application. He readily accepted, not that he had any choice in the matter anyway. The night was still young, and there were lost conjugal grounds to make up.

12

Wally's restaurant served as a sort of community center. It was centrally located in the heart of the neighborhood. There was a bulletin board near the entrance where all and comers placed various notices, from funeral dates to school bazaars. Mr. Washington was devoted to the community, and they reciprocated with their patronage. Although business was heavy every day, Friday and Saturday evenings were the busiest. Mr. Washington enjoyed playing host to his customers. He moved his massive frame around nimbly with the agility of an Olympic gymnast. He would be in one corner, asking Mrs. Weaver about her sore leg, and the next moment would see him in another corner, handing out candies to Mr. Davis's grandson. He particularly relished pointing out how fast little Shawn was growing; his food worked wonders for the body. He would joke, clown, console, encourage, or offer words of wisdom to anyone. He was the epitome of a happy and successful entrepreneur. When Osaru bade him good night in the early hours of Saturday, that was the picture he had of him in his mind. As he left, Mr. Washington was having a drink and watching television, looking very content and without a worry in the world.

The telephone rang insistently. He checked the time on his alarm radio clock; it was a few minutes before seven in the morning. It was a Sunday morning, the only day he could afford to sleep late, and now this call. It better be important, he swore under his breath as he disentangled himself from Yolanda's grip. The voice was authoritative, almost grave. Could he come to the restaurant to identify Mr. Washington's body? The plethora of police cars and wailing sirens of ambulances confirmed that the call was no hoax. Mr. Washington had been shot twice in the head at close range. He died immediately. Detectives, fingerprint experts, coroners, and others swamped all over. There was no forced entry; apparently, the perpetrator was a familiar person, they said. The detectives wanted to know when he last saw Mr. Washington, what he did after he left the restaurant, if they had any arguments or disagreements, any resentment or lingering animosity. What about Yolanda? Did she leave home at any time last night? Was she the heiress to the deceased? Was there a life insurance? If he did not know better, he would have thought that the detectives suspected that Yolanda or himself had something to do with Mr. Washington's death. He was incensed, and Yolanda was convulsing in anger. They apologized but insisted that they must explore all avenues of inquiry; close family members were routinely questioned in homicides of this nature. They continued. Did Mr. Washington have any enemies, people he resented or who resented him, any business associates or friends? As for friends, he told the detectives that practically included everybody in the neighborhood, but he knew of no enemies. For Yolanda, it was the end of the world. She was hysterical and inconsolable. The only parent she ever knew was gone. She cried herself hoarse and refused to eat or talk to anybody.

Arranging Mr. Washington's funeral would have been daunting but for the assistance of his church members. After a sedate and elegant service, Mr. Washington was interred alongside his wife, Niki, Yolanda's mother. As they left the cemetery, a middle-aged man introduced himself as Brandon, Mr. Washington's attorney, slipped out his business card, and invited them to his office within the week to read Mr. Washington's will.

Mr. Washington left a small fortune for Yolanda. He gave her nearly everything he owned—the restaurant, his house, two hundred thousand dollars in his savings account, life insurance, and other personal items. A codicil to the Will gave Osaru a 25 percent interest in the restaurant. The will considerably improved Yolanda's spirit. She even booked an appointment with her hair stylist. The greatest sign of her distress was her hair. She had not done anything to or with it since her father's death, and that was a whole week!

The restaurant was gradually getting back to normal, although flowers and cards of condolences still trickled in. The restaurant's account was always in a state of perpetual flux, between deposits and withdrawals. After three visits to the bank with an attorney, Yolanda and Osaru replaced Mr. Washington as signatories to the account. It would have been impossible in the interim to keep the restaurant afloat but for the kind gesture of suppliers, who granted a period of grace to pay their bills.

Every evening, he sat on Mr. Washington's chair to balance the books. It was always disappointing to him. After paying bills, taxes, and wages, there was hardly anything left. The figures were staggering to him. How could they make so much money and not make profits? Sometimes they actually operated at a loss. He had to cut costs. He imposed a series of austerity measures—reduce energy use, more ice and less soda, thin bread for sandwich, less onions, pickles on demand only, and more. Despite his best efforts, the financial health of the restaurant was still dire. How did Mr. Washington do it so well? he kept asking himself. The patronage was still heavy; in fact he thought that it increased since his death. He had made the restaurant more youth friendly, created a children's playroom, and reduced the size of the "monster burger" to the small but more affordable "hip burger." His experiment with a pay phone was abandoned soon after its introduction because it attracted gang members to the front of the restaurant.

Yolanda was not particularly helpful or sympathetic to the problems of the restaurant. She showed no interest in its management except its finances. She had been on a shopping binge since she cashed her inheritance. The only problem was that she did not seem to make the connection between the amount on the check and the actual amount in the bank. Invariably, he had to make up the difference and the obligatory bank fees for insufficient funds. They now lived in Mr. Washington's estate; it was spatial and palatial, and so was the mortgage. He tried to persuade her into selling the mansion and moving into a smaller and more affordable house, but she would not hear it. The house was her heritage, she said, and she would not part with it. Since her father's death, she had become very fatalistic. She would end every argument about money and austerity with "Where is my dad today? He made all the money and lived a frugal life. I will not make the same mistake. I will live well while I am alive."

It was well past midnight, and he was going through the employers' payroll and sales tax figures sent in by the accountant. They were due in three days, and from his projections and bank statements, he was going to be a couple thousand dollars short. If only Yolanda was more frugal, they would at least have something in their personal account. He would try the bank in the morning; maybe they would be helpful, although he had his doubts. He heard or read something about redlining somewhere. Redlining meant that banks simply refused to loan money to businesses or individuals in some neighborhoods. Subjects of the policy cried racism; the banks pleaded unqualified applicants. He would find out in the morning.

He was locking the file cabinet when he thought he heard a sound. The last employee left some thirty minutes earlier. Then he heard a more distinct and unmistakable sound; he turned and froze as two men in black leather jackets and pants motioned him to his seat with guns trained on him. It was well past midnight, but they wore sunglasses. Mr. B wanted a word with him, they announced. He did not know a Mr. B; he certainly frowned at his means of invitation. Just then a rather-large thickset man walked in. He was impeccably dressed in a silk suit with matching shoes and tie. He may have unorthodox visiting habits, but he was given to sartorial elegance. He spoke in an authoritative baritone. His eyes peered right into Osaru's, and he thought he looked like villains in movies capable of the most heinous crimes. He was paralyzed with fear. Would he meet the same fate as Mr. Washington? He should have listened to Yolanda, who kept warning him about keeping late hours. Oh, his poor mother. How would she take his death? He was certainly not a saint, but he did not deserve a violent death at the peak of his life. Then Mr. B waved off his escorts and apologized for intruding, but he had an urgent matter that could not wait that was better discussed under the cover of darkness. Just then the telephone rang and he reached to answer it, but Mr. B stopped him.

"Nobody should know I am here," he instructed. It was Yolanda demanding to know why he was working later than usual. She was cold and urged him to "hurry home and make me a happy wife." If only she knew. He assured her that he would be on his way immediately. He hoped his shaky voice had not given away his anxiety. He apologized to Mr. B; it was his wife, he explained. Mr. B, the gracious guest, said he took no offense. He was married too and understood, and by the way, he was not Mr. B; he was only Mr. B's emissary. Mr. B did not make house calls. Of course not, he replied, as if he well understood the protocol of the underworld. How important of him to expect a visit from Mr. B. If this was a mere emissary for Mr. B's, then he did not want to confront the real Mr. B.

"Mr. B brings you greetings. He proposes to lease your restaurant after business hours for two hours a night. For your trouble, you get ten thousand dollars a month."

"Why does he need the restaurant at such odd hours?"

"Mr. B does not take kindly to asking about his business?"

"I will need to know. Further, he will need to sign a lease prepared by my attorney prohibiting use for illegal purposes, providing for insurance coverage, damages, and the like."

"Perhaps I did not make myself clear." Raising his voice, he said, "Mr. B wants the use of this restaurant between 2:00 and 4:00 a.m. daily. Now, that is the lease. No further questions. We expect a positive response tomorrow." With that he got up, headed toward the door, stopped midway, turned around, and said, "Mr. B sends his condolences about your father-in-law. He was a nice man who got greedy." Osaru slumped into his chair with a knot in his stomach, a migraine in his head, and a quivering jaw.

Yolanda was lying on the couch, covered in a bedsheet, when he got home. As soon as he got close to her, she flung the sheet off, revealing a red-and-black embroidery lingerie that left little to the imagination. Yolanda was a well-proportioned woman and filled out every crank of the attire. If only she knew. He collected himself on the drive home and resolved not to tell her about the incident with Mr. B's emissary or whoever he was. She would be too hysterical and might do a stupid thing like going to the police. Then, Mr. B would happily kill everybody. He had done it once, or at least his emissary implied he had, and he had no reason to think he would not do it again. This was a delicate situation that demanded tact and skillful handling. After all, his people say that it is with care and cunning that you kill a mouse trapped inside your clay pot without breaking the pot itself. He tried to put her off; he was ill, he had a headache, and his leg was sore. Nothing worked. This was a determined woman. She methodically took off his clothes and proceeded to massage his shoulders. Reluctantly and against his inner feelings, his body started to respond. Well, to fool her, he had to play along, and in any case, he was enjoying it. Whatever harm awaited him was not due till the morning. As they lay on the floor like the exhausted combatants that they were, he impulsively asked, "Do you know Mr. B?"

Not really, she replied, but had heard about him in the neighborhood. He was feared and talked about in hushed tones. Why did he ask?

"Nothing," he replied. "Someone mentioned him in a conversation. Did he know your dad?"

"I do not know, but he must have heard about him. But why?"

"Nothing."

"Do not hide anything from me. What is it, baby? We are in this together. Come on, baby. What is it?" she demanded.

"Nothing, I swear. Someone just mentioned him in passing, nothing to it," he maintained.

"You sure about that?" she persisted.

"Yes."

"Then tell me why you looked like death when you walked in. Where was your bubbling, grinning self when you came in? Take a look at yourself in the mirror. You look like you have seen a ghost. If you are going to keep secrets from me, you better learn to sleep alone. You will sleep on the couch till you can trust me."

After many protestations and several overt and subtle threats from her, he relented and told her everything about his encounter with Mr. B's emissary.

"So he killed my dad?" she asked, teary-eyed. They sat still holding each other for a long time. "I am scared," she finally said between snivels. "I am scared for you," she told him. "Everybody I ever loved, I have lost. My mother, she died before I knew her. My biological father, I did not know him either. My stepfather was taken just when I was old enough to appreciate him and all he did for me. They are after you, the only one I have."

"I can take care of myself," he assured her. "I just wanted to protect you. Do not get involved in this. I will handle this alone."

"So what do you intend to do?" she asked.

"They want an answer tomorrow. I have to figure it out tonight."

"Baby, I am so scared. Those are bad people, very bad people who would do anything to achieve their goals."

They discussed every possibilities—call the police, sell the restaurant and skip town, tell Mr. B to leave them alone.

"Before I forget, they are willing to pay ten thousand dollars a month for use of the restaurant." He noted that the figures seemed to impress her, but she was suspicious and asked why they were willing to pay that much for limited use.

"They could lease any building for less," she observed.

"That is the catch. They do not want any written lease, just a verbal understanding. In their line of business, paper trails must be avoided." They talked through most of the night with no acceptable solution in sight.

The telephone rang; it was still early morning, and they probably had been asleep for a couple of hours. The phone rang a few more times; he hoped it would stop, but it persisted. Reluctantly he picked it up and growled, his displeasure evident in his "Hello." The voice was unmistakably that of Mr. B's assistant.

"Nobody knows about our discussion, right?" Before he could answer, he continued, "Will see you tonight, same time. By the way, Ms. Beasley does a nice job on Yolanda's hair every Wednesday at 12:30 p.m. We do not want any mistakes in that regard. Do we?" He hung up. His mind was made up. They could do whatever they desired provided Yolanda was not hurt. Protecting her was his primary responsibility. He would do everything in his power, albeit limited as it is, to ensure no harm came to her.

It was a Wednesday, Yolanda's hair day. He tried to talk her out of keeping the appointment, to no avail.

"It will be next week before I get another slot. My hair will be funky by then," she protested. No need to press further; it would only arouse her suspicion. Hopefully, Mr. B would hold fire until he heard his answer. A wiry smile came to his lips. His naivety astonished even himself. How could he know what these fellows would or would not do? It was foolish to expect these people to play fair. He was adhering to cricket rules in an alley fight!

Yolanda expressed her apprehensions about dealing with Mr. B but saw no viable alternative. As she put it, "We are damned if we do and damned if we don't," a variant of her newly acquired fatalistic doctrine. Yolanda was not one to give up a fight simply for fear of defeat; she was going to make it interesting somehow. "We have to show them that we have some backbone," she argued. "Tell them they can have the restaurant for twenty thousand a month, or else they can find someone else to intimidate." He thought she was joking at first, but her square jaw and the distant, lost look in her eyes portrayed otherwise. Knowing Yolanda, she probably recognized the danger but saw an opportunity to satisfy her shopping addiction. She was a true believer in pleasure now, pain later, if ever. Accordingly, he began his relationship with Mr. B, or more appropriately, Mr. B's emissary, first in fright then cautiously and later indifference.

13

To his amazement, Mr. B's emissary agreed to pay twenty thousand dollars with little or no argument. No receipts were necessary. They needed the restaurant for just a couple of hours a night. They left no trash behind, in fact no trace that they were ever there. They were despicable but ruthlessly efficient; he had to give them that. He often wondered the nature of their activities after his departure in the night. He prayed he never had to find out.

Mr. B's money was a lifeboat. He promptly paid all his bills and had more than enough left over to cover Yolanda's extravagant checks. She had recently discovered that she could save herself the commute by shopping at home through television and on the Internet. For her, online shopping was the greatest invention since sliced bread. She had become so regular on the television shopping network that the hosts identified her by first name only; "Yolanda from Dallas," they would flatter her. She enjoyed the thrill daily, and he was not about to interfere and risk a domestic war. Experience had thought him to pick his fights, only those he could win and she could afford to lose. Shopping was not one of them.

One day, the restaurant's kitchen ventilating system broke down, effectively rendering any kitchen activity impossible. He promptly replaced the entire unit. Prior to Mr. B's lease, if he could call it that, an incident of that nature would have sent them to the bankruptcy court.

Yolanda was happy, relaxed, and very supportive. They planned a vacation for the summer in the Bahamas. It suddenly dawned on him that he could not travel out of the country without first regularizing his stay. It was a perfect time to broach the subject with Yolanda again. She was very agreeable, especially because their vacation abroad hinged on it. The attorney went through the same routine as their prior visit but informed them that the unprecedented increase in the number of applicants made it well-nigh impossible for him to obtain his resident permit before their scheduled vacation date. Emergency travel documents were available only for emergency situations like serious illness or death in the family. Yolanda argued that their situation was an emergency. The attorney agreed but added that the immigration service would, in all certainty, disagree with her characterization.

For days, Yolanda was despondent; she had looked forward to the Caribbean trip, eagerly broadcasting it to her friends. Las Vegas would be a good substitute, he implored her. She was skeptical at first. Could he travel to Las Vegas without the documents? Was it not too hot over there? And in any case, she did not like gambling. Finally, she warmed up to the idea and embraced it with religious zeal. The papers could wait until after their vacation.

Yolanda had never flown before. She was apprehensive, she said, because she had seen too many sad newscasters finishing a sentence about a plane crash with "There were no survivors." He tried to reassure her about the relative safety of air travel compared to other forms of transportation. She scoffed at his statistics and theory of aerodynamics.

"How did you intend to get to the Bahamas?" he asked in frustration.

"Cruise ship," she answered. They bantered back and forth on the subject before she reluctantly agreed to fly.

She wore her heart on her sleeve throughout the flight, rising and sinking with every turn, bump, ascension, or descension. It was a relief when the plane finally taxied to a stop.

Las Vegas, by design and purpose, was constructed to take advantage of human vices and weaknesses. The entire city was a giant slot machine designed to send visitors home broke and begging to come back for more. When they left a week later, their credit cards had maxed out. A television sage once counseled not to leave home without them; they sure were life savers.

A month after their vacation, Osaru, settled back into his work routine, was rounding up for the day when Mr. B's emissary appeared in his customary manner in his office, late and uninvited. It had been six months since he last heard from them. They just left the rent, if it could be called that, in cash under his chair at the end of the month. He feigned his pleasure at meeting the emissary but was terrified inwardly. He was very brief and precise. Mr. B had directed that five million dollars be wired from a Swiss offshore bank directly into the restaurant account. He was to withdraw the same in four equal installments after seven days. For his trouble, he would get one hundred thousand dollars. He protested; the large sum would invite suspicion, and the law would trace the source of the money.

"Mr. B knows people," he replied without explanation and was gone.

Why did Mr. B not deposit the money into his own account? Because the source of the funds was illegal or at least questionable. They even knew his bank account number. Nothing was sacred anymore, he concluded. Well, he had no choice but go along for the ride to a destination he knew would be unpleasant. Yolanda did not need to know this; she would be too blinded by the shopping potentials to recognize the risks.

As promised, they delivered the hundred thousand in crisp hundred-dollar bills after the last withdrawal. He had never seen so much money in his life as he had seen in the previous two weeks. The restaurant had become very profitable. Their private account was getting fatter by the day. He bought himself a new car and opened a separate secret account with his new fortune. His wardrobe was drab, so he spared no expense for a makeover. They were at last a happy couple; life could not be better.

He was making his rounds through the restaurant one day when he noticed a strikingly beautiful young woman quietly nibbling at her salad. He stopped and said hello. He would have sworn that he had seen her before, perhaps on a television commercial or a music video. They chatted about the heat, vacation, the ongoing celebrity trial, and more. He slipped the fact of his proprietorship into the conversation, and she complimented him for the food. He wanted to stay, but there was nothing more to say, so he made his excuse and left. He sat in his office, trying to concentrate on paperwork, but could not get her out of his mind. He should have asked for her telephone number. Well no, he did the right thing. He was married. Yolanda would probably kill him if he cheated on her. He scolded himself for his teenage impulses. With all the fatal sexual diseases around, it was prudent for him to keep his sword in his sheath. He had been faithful for all of the two years of their marriage. In the last six months, he had been tempted several times but resisted because he had enough trouble as it was. Further, he loved his wife. He did the right thing, he told himself. Just then, there was a knock on the door, and she walked in. It was the lady in the restaurant, radiant, elegant, tall, alluring, and inviting. He stood up more out of shock and nervousness than courtesy.

"I do not mean to intrude," she said, "but I thought I will leave my number in case you want to talk sometime."

"That is very gracious of you," he replied. There was an awkward silence.

"I must be leaving," she announced. He protested half-heartedly.

"Stay a while," he urged her. "Have a seat, a drink." What a bad host he was. She refused and was gone with her trailing voice, saying, "Call me."

Verma was her name. His antennae for danger was on full alert. He was courting disaster. Yolanda would kick him out of the house at best—that is, if she did not shoot him first. He would not call her, he resolved. He had been faithful, and there was no reason to stray now. On the other hand, it would only be an affair, and if Yolanda did not find out, no harm was done. He would continue to love Yolanda unequivocally, but what if she found out? For two days, he tormented himself with the pros and cons of an affair outside marriage. Twice he stopped after dialing the first three numbers. Maybe he was overreacting. Nothing had happened yet. He may have been reading too much into her gesture, which may be entirely innocent; she may even reject him anyway. She was pleased to hear from him. He was a gentleman for keeping his promise. She worked for a sports-promotions outfit and traveled extensively. Studied marketing at Berkeley, California, and had lived in Dallas for four years, although she was originally from Louisiana. They talked on the phone like long-lost high school sweethearts. Throughout their conversation, he put her on hold several times to take incoming calls; this time it was Yolanda, calling to remind him to sign some documents for a new television satellite equipment she wanted.

When he came back on the line with Verma, she said, "You are a busy man. I do not want to take your time. I have two tickets to the basketball game. You know his 'Airness' makes his annual trip to town on Saturday. Want to come?" He accepted without thinking. He was a basketball fan and especially of the game's most gifted and celebrated player, Art Rivers. He was reverently referred to as Airness because of his gravity-defying acrobatics. His once-a-year trip to the city was a rite of passage for both devotees and casual followers. The fact that the local team was perpetually in the cellar of the league made this the only game of the season to cause some stir among sports fans. An opportunity to see his royal Airness in company of Verma was too good an offer to turn down.

The fast pace of their relationship surprised and worried him. He was comfortable and relaxed with her as if they had known each other forever. She sort of relished the discreet nature of their relationship. She would call his private number in the office and hang up immediately. He would call her back, and they would talk about odds and ends and arrange their next meeting.

Every so often, he received mails inviting him to various conferences at exotic locations. Every group, it seemed, got hold of his name—the minority restauranteurs, minority entrepreneurs, associations of restaurant owners, small business owners, and more. They all, for a small fee, would be glad to have him as a conferee. He had always trashed such correspondence without paying too much attention until he met Verma. He started to take more interest in the out-of-town conferences. She tailored her business travels around his conferences. They concocted elaborate schemes to avoid each other before or at the airport and united only in the safety of the plane. He enjoyed these trips thoroughly. For once he never had to make nervous glances above his shoulders, expecting Yolanda to jump out any minute. Verma was the consummate tourist. She could figure out a place fast and read maps like an air traffic controller. As soon they arrived in a city, she would lay out their itinerary. Rarely, if ever, did he attend any conference; he merely collected brochures and souvenirs. To placate his guilt, he would buy expensive and multiple gifts for Yolanda.

Some months ago, he observed that Yolanda's shopping bills were surprisingly low, in fact lower than his! She had a new passion now, motherhood. She wanted to be a mother; she wanted more than anything else to have a baby. This was a new and surprising development to him. She had never struck him as particularly maternal or displaying any proclivity for motherhood. She was serious, she said. Thus started months of visits to various doctors. Sex was different when the definite objective was procreation. Whatever happened to youth? After an evening with Verma, the nights with Yolanda were not exactly thrilling. He did his best to feign interest, but it became harder and harder to stroke his fire. She would complain, cajole, implore, and cry to no avail. He was no longer the man he used to be, she would say in frustration.

She was now very unhappy and snapped at the slightest provocation. The baby stuff was getting to her. Anytime she saw a baby, her face would light up; she would wrest it from the mother, caress it, drool, and kiss it all over. He had to do something. He suggested artificial insemination. The doctors said they were a perfectly healthy couple and, in the normal course of things, should have no problems having babies. Since her patience was running out, it was time to take advantage of all new advances science had to offer. She was cool to the idea initially but was reassured by her doctor that it was relatively safe. She agreed to try a clinic in Alabama. Their appointment was about a month away. The clinic sent a large volume of literature and had a twenty-four-hour hotline. Their role, as they explained it, was minimal; they merely fertilized and incubated eggs from parents and replanted the same in the mother. There was no third-party involvement, and the success rate was 90%.

14

He had a date with Verma, and as was their wont, they planned to spend the evening at a plush restaurant and retire to her place, where they would sip wine and listen to jazz music. When she was particularly pleased with him, she would dance to the music and strip tease. Her perfectly sculptured body gyrating nimbly was a sight to behold. She was so caring, loving, and considerate. So perfect, so beautiful. Was he falling in love with her? What about Yolanda? What if she found out? The penalty was death; he had no doubt about that. He was conflicted. He knew that their anonymous affairs could not continue much longer, at least not the status quo. Verma would no sooner demand more. Being a mistress had its thrills, she once remarked casually, but having someone to call your own exclusively was, in the long run, more satisfying. He had been taken aback, being totally unprepared for her serious side. She had always been a happy-go-lucky girl. Yolanda, on the other hand, although none the wiser, would invariably sniff out telltale signs of infidelity. She already teased him now as a lady's man in mock indignation before he left home for work. She complimented his newly acquired sartorial taste and admonished him not to take the ladies' compliments to heart. If she ever found out, well . . . .

It was a Friday evening. He had lunch with Yolanda earlier and was looking forward to seeing Verma that evening. She had been out of town for the week on an assignment to Toronto. The basketball league was going international by establishing franchises in Canada. Her company would be a big player in marketing the upstart teams. Try as much as he did, he could not get out of the restaurant on time.

A phone call here, signature there, someone stopping by to say hello, the pastor dropping in to remind him of the youth-revival donations. When he eventually extricated himself, he barely had fifteen minutes to drive across town to her apartment. He was driving against the flow of traffic; with any luck, he would be only a few minutes late. He had recently discovered a new easy listening radio station that played adult contemporary music continuously with little or no talk. The song was fairly familiar, and he hummed along while pushing the accelerator a little harder. He thought he heard a siren but was not quite sure. It may have been an ambulance racing to one emergency or the other. He could not understand why the accident rate was high in this country despite the wide and smooth roads. Good thing these people did not drive on the death traps used as roads in his country. Now the wailing of the police siren was unmistakable. The flashing light and haunting sound was directly behind him. He signaled and pulled over.

Well, in his hurry, he had forgotten his wallet, which contained his driver's license and insurance card. With little ceremony, the policeman gave him tickets for exceeding the speed limit, driving without a license, and the lack of proof of insurance.

These were minor infractions that his attorney would straighten out. About time his attorney started earning his keep. He decided to return to the restaurant, call Verma to explain, and cancel their date or see her later in the day. He had just walked into the restaurant when a plainclothes officer informed him he was under arrest and read him his Miranda rights, essentially an advisory to shut up while you can. There was a Drug Enforcement Agency (DEA) hold on him, whatever that meant. Outside, the wailing and shrieking of alarm from a plethora of police cars warned him that there was a major problem, reminiscent of the morning of Mr. Washington's death.

At the big tall brown brick building downtown, he was booked in after an inventory of his personal items and fingerprints were taken. He was then led to a small cell that already had one occupant. Could he make a call? No, the inmates' pay phone was out of order. They would see what they could do. If only he could call Yolanda;

Brandon, his attorney; and Verma in that order, he could then adjust to his new environment, safe in the belief that he had committed no crimes and all the fuss was due to mistaken identity. Was he really blameless? What of the money transfer on behalf of Mr. B? He was now less confident. Mr. B had assured him that all would be well. He was a fool for trusting that thug, but did he have a choice? He had not taken religion seriously in a long time; he needed prayers now, but would it be helpful? His high school principal often said that the Lord would not umpire a game between two devils. He was now in a dance with the devil and had lost any right to divine intervention. Yolanda would be worried to death if he did not contact her somehow. Verma would understand and perhaps make jokes about it when he explained his predicament.

The cell was a cold, nondescript small room. The toilet was right there, near the bed! It made his stomach turn. There was already a lone occupant who was lying on the single bed and apparently did not want to be disturbed. His anxiety was relieved by the faint hope that his only identifiable illegality were the traffic violations that usually invited minor sanctions. The police, he assured himself, were overreacting. When they calmed down, they would realize their error and set him free. As the minutes turned into hours, he became apprehensive and even desperate. His cell mate was now snoring loudly, apparently indifferent to his environment. There were clangs of iron doors, bangs on the same, and harrowing noise from other inmates at regular intervals. A tray containing two dishes were pushed into the cell some hours later. He was too angry and disgusted to eat. His cell mate promptly woke up and ate both dishes with his permission. The guy appeared very comfortable. Osaru admired him. He was making the best of his circumstances. Unlike him, who was still in denial and could not understand why he was in jail. His knowledge of jail life was restricted to the horror stories he heard or read about. So far, this was a quiet cell. His cell mate behaved more like a sleep-deprived vacation guest.

He must have slept in a sitting position because he was awakened by the crank of the iron door. It was already morning when he was taken to a front room, where a Judge was sitting. There were few other inmates there. The judge, whom they called a magistrate for some reason, granted him bail. He signed some documents and was released on bail, but he first had to accompany some agents to a search of his restaurant and home. The search warrant had just been signed by a judge. At the lobby, Yolanda and his attorney, Brandon, were waiting. Yolanda rushed and held on to him. He felt undeserving. If only she knew where he was headed when all this happened.

She had rushed to the restaurant and taken over last night. She had called his attorney, who assured her he would be all right. Brandon had arranged bail after she paid fifteen thousand dollars.

"Fifteen thousand dollars for a traffic ticket!" Brandon explained that he was being held for drug trafficking. This must be a joke, he insisted. He protested his innocence. He had never seen cocaine in his life; there must have been a mistake; Brandon would clear this up in no time. Brandon's reaction was unsettling. He had the quizzical look of disbelief, as if saying, "I have heard that before." Yolanda was more comforting; she had not slept all night. She was just grateful he was alive. She was afraid of losing him.

"Whatever it is baby, we will beat it."

It was still hazy and misty in the morning, that time of the morning when everything was still a silhouette, when he arrived at the restaurant. There were a battery of marked and unmarked police cars swarming all around. The search was in progress; they were thorough but nonintrusive. The restaurant's first shift worked gingerly around the officers and their dogs. They combed every nook and corner of the property—the walls, ceilings, drawers, store, picture frames, everything. The more they came up empty, the more determined they seemed to be. They appeared confident that it would only be a matter of time before they struck gold. At about midday, most of the contingent left except for a skeletal crew who now moved to the open space behind the restaurant. The dogs were sniffing all over the place. Then one of the dogs became very restless and furiously dug at a particular spot; the others joined. The beam of satisfaction on the faces of their handlers indicated that their perseverance had paid off at last. They dug at the spot, which quickly revealed a flat wooden board with a doorknob. It actually looked like a small window. They lifted it, revealing a dark concrete tunnel below. Big flashlight on hand, one of them climbed in. The tunnel at first was narrow and snakelike but soon opened into a large space filled with rows of boxes. It was cocaine.

At a hearing before a judge later that day, bail was revoked. According to the prosecutor, he was a drug baron with international connections and posed a very high flight risk. It took two weeks, another hearing, the confiscation of his travel passport, fifty thousand dollars, and the wearing of an electronic monitor on his ankle to secure his release. For two weeks, he was placed in solitary confinement because he was classified as extremely dangerous and posed maximum risk. The cell was a dark windowless concrete and iron fortress. He was locked up twenty-three hours a day and let out in shackles for one hour. He looked forward to his one hour of relative freedom a day. He was usually marched through a well-lit corridor into a small field, where he could hear other inmates but could not see them. The smell of the wet grass, insect noise, or human voices now carried a special significance for him. The ancient philosopher was right. A man is a man only in the context of society; a man outside society was either a beast or a god.

He spent some of his time reading the Bible, which from the endorsement on the first page was donated by a Christian group. He was shocked at the number of wars and level of relative cruelty and destruction in the Old Testament. He wondered if they had solitary confinements then; perhaps they did since most crimes then commanded the death penalty.

He often thought about his mother and sister. How were they now? What if they knew he was in jail for drug trafficking! They probably would not understand the gravity of the crime. Drugs like cocaine were still relatively unknown when he left home. He remembered the bedtime stories his mother told when he was a kid. It usually ended with a song. His favorite was the "King's Daughter and the Pauper's Son."

The king's daughter was the most beautiful maiden in the entire "world." Suitors from far and near came to ask for her hand in marriage, and she rejected them all. One day she went to the river for a swim. As she descended the hill sloping into the river, she saw a handsome young man diving into the river and outswimming every other competitor. As was the custom, everyone cleared the river to enable the princess to swim uncontaminated and undisturbed by commoners. The young man passed by and saluted in her praise name, Imose, "one whose looks hypnotizes." She smiled and he smiled back. She almost fainted; his smile was electric. She made inquiries and started seeing the young man secretly every evening under the big tree near the palace. She had been warned by her servants that the young man was the son of the village pauper.

"Your father, the king, will execute him and his father if he finds out," they warned her. At about the same time, the king of a neighboring community came to ask for the princess's hand in marriage to his son, the prince, heir apparent to his throne. They brought lots and lots of gifts for the prince and her father, the king. The young prince was bedecked in expensive gold chains, coral beads, and ivory. He looked every inch like the future king of a prosperous community. The king was impressed; at last, he had found a worthy suitor for his daughter. After the feast, as was the custom, the prince had to formally ask for the princess's hand in marriage. Everyone assumed that this was a mere formality; with the display of such opulence, wealth, and splendor, who could turn down the young prince? The princess, instead of simply and coyishly answering yes, as was expected, broke into a song:

> You may wear all the gold in the world.
> You can own all the silver in the world.
> You may even own the air I breathe.
> But I have made up my mind.
> This is the one for me!

As she sang the last line, she danced into the crowd and held on to the pauper's son. His mother's voice still rang in his ears as she sang those lines as if they held personal significance for her. Did she make up those stories to build their self-esteem, that their material deprivation did not necessarily foreshadow an unsuccessful life? He could never tell, but even now, those stories remained a fountain of inspiration for him. One of the changes he resolved to make when he was through with his legal problems was take better care of his mother and sister. Although he had written occasionally and had been generous to them financially, he knew he could never do enough for them.

15

Jury selection had just begun. On the advice of his attorney, he wore a conservative blue pin-striped suit, a white shirt, and a rather-bland tie.

"Nothing flashy," he had been warned. "You do not want the jury thinking that you are flaunting your wealth." He also imposed a no-jewelry-except-wristwatch rule. He took a look at himself in the mirror and was impressed. He looked like an accountant. He had almost forgotten that he was indeed an accountant!

The presiding judge was introduced, or rather announced, to the court by a hefty-looking man as the Honorable Theresa Cornell. The prosecutors also introduced themselves, all five of them. It was his attorney's turn. Brandon, like everyone else, obsequiously introduced himself and his associate, a stunningly beautiful lady, whom he thought should be reading the evening news on television or catcalling on Broadway. He was introduced, and the jurors were informed that he was on trial for drug trafficking.

The lead prosecutor, Jerome Abramson, was rather self-effacing and deceptively understated. He thanked the jurors for taking time off their busy schedules to honor the call of the court. Society was grateful to responsible citizens such as they were for their invaluable service to the community. He hoped that the five-dollar-a-day honorarium they would receive would not be interpreted as a measure of their work's worth but as a token of their selflessness. They were assembled to determine whether the man, pointing to Osaru, was guilty or not guilty of the crime charged in the indictment. Did they know that in criminal proceedings, the law required the facts to be established beyond reasonable doubt? What did that mean? Did any of them know? Some volunteered answers; he commended their efforts and continued his lecture.

"'Beyond reasonable doubt' does not mean beyond every shadow of a doubt. Otherwise, only confessions and perhaps video tapes will suffice for convictions, and as we have seen in recently well-publicized trials, even those may be insufficient. In civil cases, the law requires a balance of probability. What does this mean? Which standard is higher and more difficult to attain?"

The group chorused their answer, "Beyond reasonable doubt."

"That is correct. 'Beyond reasonable doubt' merely means that a reasonable person, looking at the totality of the evidence, will conclude that the facts support a guilty verdict. It does not mean that you have to have a mathematical certitude or that you do not have any doubts whatsoever but that a reasonable person will conclude that the facts support a finding of guilt." He continued his didactic presentation until yawns from the jurors compelled the judge to suggest that it was high time he wrapped up. Mercifully he complied. Brandon took off where the prosecutor stopped.

"As the prosecutor rightly told you, there are different standards of proof for criminal and civil cases. One requires proof beyond reasonable doubt. The other mandates a preponderance of the evidence. We are all agreed that the criminal standard is higher. Why do you suppose that is?" After several suggestions from a number of jurors, a middle-aged lady sitting on the last row said, "Because a citizen's freedom is at stake." Brandon found the answer he was expecting and shouted "Exactly" with the enthusiasm of a schoolteacher who had finally made a complicated and subtle point to his class. "Our forefathers rightly concluded that a citizen's freedom should not be taken lightly. They therefore imposed this procedural safeguards so that the state can only use its powers *ex abundanti cautela,* out of abundant caution. Whereas in civil matters, the law merely requires a preponderance of the evidence—that is, if you are satisfied that more likely than not, a set of facts has been proven. On the other hand, a mere hunch or suspicion that a certain state of facts exists is insufficient to ground a criminal conviction. The state must prove beyond a reasonable doubt, not subjectively but through an objective standard of reasonableness, that the defendant committed the act alleged by the prosecution.

"Further, the defendant does not have to do anything. In fact, the defendant does not have to say anything or take the stand to defend himself, and you cannot use that fact against him. The onus is on the prosecution to prove its case beyond reasonable doubt. This is not a question of fairness or a level playing field but a matter of constitutional guarantee." He spoke for a fairly long time. Osaru had never seen Brandon in court. He had newfound respect for him. He had always seen him as a dapper attorney who hung an unlit cigar perpetually on his lips. He had become Osaru's lawyer simply because he had inherited him as Mr. Washington's lawyer and knew a lot about the restaurant's business.

The *voir dire*—that was what they called the process of jury selection—had taken the whole day. It had its ebbs and flows—funny questions and answers, awkward moments, weird and sad moments. One lady had lost a son to drug traffickers, another thought that drugs should be legalized, a third revealed that Armageddon was upon the earth in the form of drug use.

Finally a jury of twelve and five alternates was empaneled. There appeared to be no formula to the selection. The lawyers chatted and directed questions at the potential jurors, then each side just marked out some potential jurors to be excluded—peremptory challenge, they called it—after which a jury panel emerged. There were seven women and five men. He had not noticed, but Brandon pointed out to him later that all jurors disqualified by the prosecution were black females while he excused only white males, especially those with military backgrounds.

"Never take a chance with a jury composed of military types. They are used to command structure and are natural leaders. They can get a jury to coalesce around their line of thought. Jurors are like water. They take color and shape from their environment. You always shoot for a jury you can shape their opinions. Get a jury that is a plain canvass, and you can paint anything on it." The opening address were set for the next day.

Brandon had never directly asked him about his guilt or innocence. He delicately probed around the issue in their dozen or so meetings. Two days after he was released on bond, he went to Brandon's office with Yolanda. He questioned them exhaustively on the "drug deal," as he put it. Osaru adamantly denied any knowledge of the tunnel or its content. He did not know if Mr. Washington did either. Yolanda said she grew up in the restaurant and never knew or heard about the tunnel.

His unwritten agreement with Mr. B and the money transaction were troubling. Brandon spent a considerable amount of time on this relationship. Why did Mr. B need the restaurant for a couple of hours in the early morning? Osaru was not quite sure, but given the circumstances, he had no incentive to find out. Was Mr. Washington a drug baron? Did that have anything to do with his death? Yolanda, in tears, said she thought that his death was drug related, that she had always thought of her father as an angel, but now she was not quite sure, a conclusion that completely devastated her. Osaru consoled her. Maybe her father was blackmailed into cooperation just as they were. Mr. B was a ruthless thug no could stand up to. Did she know that they had threatened to harm her if he did not cooperate? How could she be sure that the same tactic was not used on her father. She appeared to cheer up after that. Privately, Osaru, too, had his doubts. One incident stood out in his mind.

They had been married for a little over three months. It was late in the evening, and he promised Yolanda after repeated complaints to spend more time with her. His father-in-law encouraged him to work fewer hours and spend more time with his wife. According to him, women, especially new brides, wanted to be constantly assured that they were as desirable and wanted as when you first met them. The only way to show that was to spend more time together. So he went home unexpectedly. Yolanda was flustered, cagy, and edgy when he arrived. The sitting room had a thick odor of recently sprayed air freshener. When he walked toward the patio, the smell hit him—it was marijuana. At first she denied but later admitted using marijuana since high school. It was harmless, she insisted. He was speechless. Marijuana in his country was the hardest drug for a long time until cocaine started to make inroads. He was taught from infancy that marijuana caused insanity, and there was anecdotal evidence to support the claim. This, therefore, was a serious challenge to his belief system. Marijuana to him was a deadly poison, but now he was married to a woman who had used it since high school! He stormed out of the house and drove furiously back to the restaurant. Mr. Washington must hear this; he would enjoy hearing him chastise her. Her father calmly listened to him and, to his utter astonishment, asked what the fuss was about. Marijuana was a medicinal herb used by a sizable number of the population, including himself, to ease arthritis pain. The image of Mr. Washington puffing a reef of marijuana was unfathomable to him. He left with his tail between his legs.

"The state will prove that the defendant is a drug baron with connections to the mob and South American drug lords. The state will establish that the defendant has a storage of well-concealed drugs buried under his restaurant, that the restaurant was a subterfuge for operating an illegal and dangerous business. The state intends to call witnesses who will say that the defendant lived an extravagant lifestyle well beyond his means and traveled extensively throughout the country in furtherance of his illicit trade." By the time he finished, even Osaru was convinced that he was a bad and dangerous person.

Brandon spoke next. Like a mechanic, he began to reengineer the case put forth by the prosecution. Osaru was a responsible, hardworking member of the community who was in the dock only because he was a victim of circumstances. The defense would produce evidence and testimony showing that the defendant and his wife inherited the restaurant only three years ago while the tunnel was at least sixteen years old. He promised all kinds of testimony and evidence that would refute all charges alleged by the indictment. He trusted that the jurors, as honorable men and women of the community, would consider the evidence fairly.

Law enforcement officers dominated the first day of testimony. Their testimony was routine and noncontroversial as they mostly described the seizure. One aspect that pricked Osaru's interest was how the investigation was triggered. One of the police officers testified that about six months earlier, at 03:00 hours in the morning (they all referred to time in that fashion), he spotted unusual movements in and around the restaurant and, on close examination, saw a long truck at the back entrance. He noted it in his report and requested surveillance. They witnessed the same activities several times but sometimes without the long truck. Brandon had only a few questions for him, the crux of which was to get him to admit that throughout his initial and subsequent surveillance, he never saw the defendant except during normal business hours at the restaurant.

Since the trial began, he had maintained the same schedule, arriving in the court with Yolanda daily at about 8:00 a.m., dropping her off at home at the end of the day, and rushing to the restaurant to catch up with business. He particularly looked forward to going to the restaurant in the evening. Apart from being the only place he had complete control, the support he got from patrons was invigorating. The older folks bear-hugged him and prayed God to do his will and set him free. The young men were more demonstrative with their support; they would bump him with their shoulders and tell him to keep his head up and not let the "man keep you down. You gonna walk, brother." He deeply appreciated their support not only because it was unexpected but because he had anticipated that the negative publicity generated by his arraignment and trial would hurt the restaurant irreparably.

His and Mr. Washington's faces had been splashed across the front page of the only local daily under the bold caption DRUG KINGPIN NABBED. The story started with "A Nigerian drug kingpin resident in Dallas . . ." A badly tailored police mug shot of him made sinister by shades of black was placed next to stacks of cocaine. The local police chief and drug enforcement agency were beside themselves in search of superlatives to describe their haul.

The four local television stations led with the story, showing Osaru in orange prison jumpers, handcuffed and juxtaposed to the restaurant, the tunnel, and its content. He expected maximum damage from the adverse publicity and was pleasantly surprised and grateful that it did not. The media, as was their wont, had its fill in a couple of days and moved on to next victim.

The second day of testimony started out ordinarily enough. Forensic reports confirmed that the white powder found in the tunnel was indeed cocaine. Civil servants attested to the fact that the property was registered to Osaru and Yolanda. Another established that Osaru was the registered proprietor of the restaurant. A third confirmed that he signed all the tax papers. He was mildly amused at the effort to link him to the restaurant, a point he did not think was in dispute.

The court experience was new to him. Apart from television courtroom drama, he had never really been exposed to the inside workings of the court. No question, the court had a unique and distinct aura. It was cold, remote, and intimidating. The spartan, almost-ascetic furniture provided no comfort. More fascinating were the actors; the judge ("Your Honor," as they frequently addressed her) feigning perpetual sternness; court employees, who tiptoed in and out of court, except the bailiff, who looked permanently bored, and of course, the lawyers. Most Americans, he knew, were brash with the devil-may-care attitude. The obsequiousness of the lawyers to the judge was nauseating. She could virtually tell them the most disparaging thing, and they would accept it meekly without as much as a squeak. A lawyer could be making a point with the earnestness of a war marshal; one word, *overruled*, from the judge, and down he sat with his mouth shut. Where else in America could such unchallenged power and order reign? He wished her powers extended to his countrymen's association meetings, where only the threat of a machine gun ready and blazing commanded attention and order.

The pedantic and didactic nature of testimony was also infuriating to him. If one mentioned a motor vehicle, he would be required to explain. Brandon explained another puzzling rule to him. A police officer had tried to read from his notes during testimony, and Brandon objected to it. During a break, Osaru asked why.

"He cannot read from his notes in court except if we agree, but he could refresh his memory with it," he explained.

What difference did it make? he asked.

"I use the rules. I do not make them," he replied. It reminded him of a story he had read in a popular novel in high school where a man refused to offer his knife for sharing a particular type of meat because it was taboo to him but offered to use his teeth instead.

16

The afternoon session started with heated exchanges on both sides. Brandon was visibly upset. The prosecution desired to introduce a new witness not previously known to the defense. Brandon and the lead prosecutor sparred verbally on end. Finally, the judge ordered them to approach the bench for a sidebar, essentially a lawyers' conference with the judge at her desk in camera. Brandon was still livid at the sidebar, judging from his gestures. The judge ruled that the prosecution could call the witness.

"The prosecution calls Verma Adkins." He went numbed. Verma, oh no! not his Verma! There she was, radiant and vivacious as ever. He had tried several times to contact her, but her number was disconnected and her apartment vacated. The doorman, after a twenty-dollar tip, informed him that she moved out a few days earlier and left no forwarding address. He concluded that she must have believed the stories about him and decided to cut her loss while she could. If only he could explain to her. Now, there she was, in the enemy camp. With Yolanda sitting directly behind him, he could not give away his discomfort, so he struggled mightily to stay calm. Beads of perspiration soon gave him away.

"You okay, baby?" Yolanda asked.

"Yes," he lied. He now appreciated why Brandon had asked him repeatedly if he had any girlfriends. With Yolanda sitting next to him, he had been emphatic in his denial. Well, his lies were about to catch up with him.

As promised, she delivered right on cue.

"How did he know the defendant?" she was asked.

"He was my boyfriend," she answered. Yolanda turned and looked at him. Her eyes asked the question; he looked back and turned away. Two minutes into her testimony, Yolanda got up and walked away. Brandon requested and was granted a recess.

Brandon, for the first time, to put it mildly, was furious with him.

"To defend you effectively, you have to level with me. Truth is the only acceptable currency of our relationship. I am your attorney. I need to know everything to defend you effectively. Help me to help you," he cried. His assistant was about to say something, but he raised his hands and she kept quiet. The bailiff walked in; the prosecutors were seeking an audience with Brandon. He understood Brandon's anger and frustration. By now, he had probably concluded that infidelity was not the only thing he had lied about. He must reemphasize his innocence to Brandon at the earliest opportunity. The deck was stacked against him already, and a half-hearted attorney was the last thing in the world he needed.

For Yolanda, he was too afraid to think about her. He would worry about her later, but something told him to prepare for the worst. When Brandon returned a while later, he was in better spirits. The prosecutors were prepared to deal. They were offering a plea bargain, usually an agreement that allowed a defendant to plead guilty to a lesser crime or fewer charges in exchange for a lower sentence. The prosecutors were offering him the opportunity to plead guilty to possession of drugs while agreeing to drop trafficking and conspiracy charges. He must also be prepared to cooperate in locating and prosecuting his accomplices. For his trouble, he would get a five-year jail term and, according to Brandon, could be out in about three years for good behavior. What did he think? Brandon asked.

"You are the attorney. You tell me," he replied. Not surprisingly, Brandon thought it was a good deal considering the alternative, which was a possible life term on conviction and the risk of divorce if all the tabloid stuff Verma was dishing continued. "Are you saying we are bound to lose this case?" Osaru asked.

"No, but there is a high possibility," Brandon replied.

"If my attorney does not believe me, who will?"

"Look here. I am your attorney, and I love you like a brother. Given the circumstances, I will recommend accepting this deal. It is the best we can hope for, but if you reject it, I will use my last breath to defend you the best way I know how to." Osaru was adamant. He could not bring himself to pleading guilty to a crime he did not commit. Brandon used carrots and sticks; he got the prosecutors to move substantially by accepting a two-year jail term and the last three probated. His resolve was unwavering; he just could not plead guilty. The local newspaper had recently reported a crackdown on criminal aliens by the immigration authorities. The issue of criminal aliens was a hot topic in the last general elections, and Congress had passed a new legislation facilitating the deportation or removal of affected aliens. The immigration authorities were going through criminal records and deporting aliens at record numbers. The stakes were too high for him, if only Brandon could understand. This posed an existential threat to him, not just another run-of-the-mill criminal trial.

Verma was worth the price of admission. She described their relationship in painstaking details, inviting numerous objections from Brandon. He had never heard the phrase "more prejudicial than probative" used more in his life. He was feeling more relaxed now; at least she was not alleging any criminal conduct. Yes, he was unfaithful to his wife, but that was not a crime, perhaps a violation of the moral code. He read an author many years ago who argued persuasively that morality and criminality should not be confused. While they may intersect, they were not the same. He gave a particularly gory example about finding a hungry kid and refusing to feed him. While the moral code censured such a behavior, the criminal code did not. He was enjoying his philosophical excursion when Verma said something that grabbed his attention: "We traveled to all sorts of places, Florida, Arizona, New York, Las Vegas."

"What was the purpose of your travels?"

"Ostensibly for conventions and conferences."

"You said *ostensibly*. Why?"

"Because Osaru never attended any conference or seminar. He would leave in the morning and return late in the evening."

"Did the defendant ever tell you where he went?"

"Yes, he always said he was attending meetings."

"Did he tell you the type of meetings he attended?"

"No, he merely called them business meetings and that he did not want to get me in trouble. Hence, I could not attend with him."

"Did he say the kind of trouble he was talking about?"

"No, he did not elaborate, but he gave me the impression that it was for my own good not to get involved in his meetings."

"Did the defendant take anything with him to these meetings?"

"Yes, suitcases." The prosecutor brought some average-sized suitcases, and she identified one as the type she meant.

Her testimony, on its face, was damaging but circumstantial and more importantly dishonest. She had extracted innocent jovial conversations and sinisterly perverted them. He was angry and wrote notes of explanation to Brandon.

On cross-examination, she admitted that she never saw Osaru use, sell, or possess drugs of any kind and that she never heard him discussing any drug deal. She denied the suggestions that Osaru did not want her in his meetings simply to avoid being photographed with her. He could not take a chance with a photograph finding its way to his wife. She broke down when Brandon suggested that she was only an angry vindictive lover who could not get Osaru to divorce his wife to marry her. When she gathered herself, she calmly denied the suggestion and explained that her motivation was entirely altruistic. She loved him so much and was only trying to save him from himself. Cooperating with the state was the only way she could ensure that he quit his deadly trade.

He was too afraid to go home. At the restaurant, everything appeared to be normal. He stayed well past midnight before venturing home. His fears were confirmed. The front lawn was strewn with his belongings—clothes, shoes, books, boxes, warts and all. There was no use trying; he had to retreat. He picked his wares and went back to the restaurant to plot his next move. Later that night, he found a motel, which would be his home for some time. It was one of those new inns springing up all over by the day. They promised a home away from home, and on first look, it was not a shabby substitute for home.

The prosecution had wrapped up its case and Brandon was still unsure, but Osaru was importunate about his intention to testify. He had nothing to hide; truth was on his side, he insisted, to which Brandon replied, "Evidence counts more than truth in court." The matter had been made more complicated by Yolanda. She was slated as the first defense witness. Brandon had impressed it upon her that her testimony about the history of the restaurant was crucial to his defense, and it could dispense with Osaru taking the stand. She was now incommunicado. Nobody, including Brandon, could reach her. Subpoenaing her was out of the question; nobody wanted a vengeful wife as a hostile witness.

When they walked into court that morning, Yolanda was sitting in her usual spot with her aunt beside her. Aunt Maria was Yolanda's mother's only surviving sibling. She lived in a retirement community in Arizona. She was a kindhearted woman who had been a teacher for the better part of her life. She walked with a stoop, perhaps due to her height. She was taller than Osaru, who was 6'3" tall and had a penchant for wearing colorful neck beads. Her favorite words were *baby* and *Jesus*. She had two sons, one of whom never returned and was presumed dead in the war in Vietnam. The other was a real estate broker in California. He had never met him, but Aunt Maria never stopped talking about him.

Brandon was relieved to see Yolanda and quickly took her aside to go over some details. Aunt Maria told him that Yolanda called her some days earlier in great pain. She had asked her to come over and persuaded her to stay with her man in his moment of difficulty.

"Baby, the devil will tempt you in many ways. Jesus is the light, the way, and salvation. Never doubt the power of the Lord." She was an angel. Her voice was so soothing, she was so understanding, he almost cried.

When she was called to the stand, he was apprehensive. Would she use her testimony as a forum for revenge? His fears were unfounded. Her testimony was flawless. She traced the ownership and construction to her parents and described in tears the circum-stances of her father's death. No, he did not know anything about the tunnel; neither did she. He was not a drug dealer; he even detested marijuana. How did she know that? Because he said so. On cross-examination, she admitted that she did not attend any of the out-of-town conferences with him.

"If he lied to you about who he was taking with him to the conferences, could he not lie also about the nature of the business he conducted there?" Brandon jumped up as if stung by a bee and objected.

"Sustained," ruled the judge. "Disregard that question," she instructed the jury. At the end of the day, Brandon was very pleased with her performance.

Osaru expressed his gratitude as they left the court, but she ignored him. Auntie Maria counseled him to give her time.

"She is still hurting deeply. The Lord and time heal all wounds." They were going back to Arizona. She was still too fragile and traumatized to live alone in Dallas. Just before they left, Yolanda came over to Osaru and asked if they had money in their account. She needed money in exile, as she put it. Fortunately, he had deposited a large sum in the account some days earlier and was pleasantly surprised at its buoyancy. Their troubles had cured their taste for luxury. He told her to help herself generously. Brief and casual though it was, he was relieved at finally speaking to her and expressing his regrets.

Mr. Abramson, the lead prosecutor, had been delivering his closing summations for over an hour. He was armed with charts, oversized photographs, video and audiotapes, all of which he made constant references to. He contended that the state had established possession and trafficking of cocaine by the defendant, that the restaurant was a veritable warehouse for drugs and that the defendant's claim of ignorance was incredulous because of his "alleged" unwritten lease with a man he did not know and could not identify.

"Yet he eagerly leased his restaurant to this unknown fellow for use at odd hours of the night. Now, was he doing this to save his family? No, he was rewarded handsomely. For two hours a night, the defendant got twenty thousand dollars monthly. Pardon my cynicism. A deal like that will at least raise one's antennae for danger, that something was not right. What did the defendant do? Did he alert the law enforcement authorities? No, he instead pocketed the money and now throws up his hand and professes ignorance. Even if you believe the defense story, which we do not, the totality of the circumstance points irrefutably to the defendant's guilt." Pointing to the videotape he had plugged in, he continued, "The video shows the sophisticated underground tunnel below the defendant's restaurant that was used as a drug warehouse. The bales upon bales of cocaine in the video were found at the said warehouse. The street value of the seizure was estimated at about three million dollars." He rattled on and on, essentially reiterating the testimony of witnesses, the conferences, defendant's life style that could not be supported by income from the restaurant alone. The state, he concluded, had proven its case beyond reasonable doubt by showing that he was in possession of large quantities of cocaine and had traveled extensively to distribute the same. He took his seat after thanking the jurors and the judge.

Osaru surveyed the jurors to determine the efficacy of the presentation. Their bland, almost-bored expression gave away nothing. He noted, however, that two jurors scribbled away throughout the entire delivery. They appeared more interested than the others. Even they showed no outward emotions.

Brandon commenced his closing argument. He reminded the jury of their obligation to stick to the facts, not innuendos, suppositions, or hypotheses; that the burden of proof rested with the prosecution; that the prosecution must prove each charge in the indictment beyond reasonable doubt; that the defense did not have to do anything but simply challenge the prosecution to prove its case. He continued, "The law is phrased as a general proposition but must be applied to individual cases. Laws are not written to take care of a particular case. That will be illegal because it will be *ad hominem*—that is, directed at a particular individual. We submit that the elements of the crime alleged in the indictment have not been proven beyond a reasonable doubt by the prosecution." He proceeded to isolate the facts of the case piece by piece, recalling witnesses' testimonies and disposing of seemingly damning evidence with benign explanations.

After dismissing or explaining every piece of evidence the prosecution presented, he continued, "The prosecution's case appears to rest on the proposition that if you own property, any illegal item found thereon is *de facto* yours, and legal liability must flow therefrom as a matter of course. This argument was deceptively subtle but unsound. With the court's indulgence, I shall proceed to provide a historical background to this theory. The proposition that whoever owns land owns everything on top and beneath it is a property law principle of considerable antiquity. In times of yore, when mining and farming were the principal means of economic activity, land was the major means of production. The rule that possession was coterminous with ownership was imperative to place some order on land use and development. However, this rule has always been a property law, albeit a land law principle. The prosecution in this case cannot be allowed to use a civil law concept to ground a criminal conviction. Such a holding will lead to unimaginable consequences. For instance, a landowner who discovers that his land had been a mine a hundred years earlier will be liable for the content of the mine. Such an absurd result will be intolerable and unacceptable.

"In the final analysis, the prosecution's case, stripped of all its grandiosity amounts to this: that some quantity of drugs were found at an underground tunnel of the defendant's restaurant. The tunnel, from expert testimony, was at least twenty years old. The defendant had owned the restaurant for only three years. No testimony was elicited showing that the defendant knew or ought to have known of the existence of the tunnel or its content. The prosecution, lacking evidence, wants this point presumed. The law, however, does not allow this leap of faith. A crime must have two elements—physical and mental. A person must not only do a prescribed or prohibited act or omission but must also have the requisite mental element— that is, the defendant must have acted knowingly, intentionally, with reckless disregard or any other culpable state of mind. The defendant in this case was never in possession of any drugs and did not know of their existence.

"Further, the prosecution adduced no evidence to support the charge of distribution of drugs. The testimony only indicated that the defendant traveled extensively to restaurant conferences. No witness testified that they saw the defendant possess or traffic in drugs. The defendant was placed under surveillance for a considerable length of time. Neither the audio nor video recordings nor oral testimony even remotely link the defendant to drug possession or trafficking. The fact that the defendant traveled a lot cannot be extrapolated under any circumstance as supportive of the trafficking charge. The prosecution attempted to show that the defendant was unfaithful to his wife. Reprehensible as the defendant's conduct may be, the remedy lies in the civil court, and the proper complainant cannot be the state but the defendant's wife." Occasionally he would stop, sip water from a glass, adjust his reading glasses, and continue. Whenever he appeared to score a point, the spectators would hum their approval, and the judge would bring down her gavel and threaten to evacuate the court. The jury as usual was expressionless, and the two jurors scribbled away furiously. Brandon continued, "Finally, we submit that the prosecution has not proven its case beyond reasonable doubt, and we urge that the defendant be set free, but you will not be letting a guilty man off the hook, but you surely will not be sending an innocent man to jail. I thank you for your time."

Osaru was elated. Brandon had said all the things and more he would have said. Mr. Abramson had a rebuttal; it would be short, he assured the judge, who was contemplating ending the proceedings for the day. A juror had requested a half day off to attend her daughter's annual high school recital.

"Thank you, Your Honor," he commence. "The defense had attempted ingenuously to confuse the issue in this case. The prosecution knows the differences between property and criminal law. We do not assert any property law principle in this case. What we assert is what common sense dictates. Possession can either be actual or constructive. What we claim here is that the defendant had actual possession of a substantial quantity of drugs. In the alternative, even if the defense explanation is accepted, which we do not, we assert that the defendant had constructive possession because he ought reasonably to have known that his property was being used for illegal purposes but chose conveniently not to know. That is willful blindness. To hold otherwise will make prosecution virtually impossible. Every defendant will henceforth conveniently feign ignorance and point to this case. What we ask of the jury is what common sense dictates. How many average people make unwritten deals with unknown people for use of their property for a couple of hours in the early morning and get paid well above market price and not inquire into the nature of the tenant's activity? The answer to that question should guide your decision. I thank you very much."

The jury had deliberated for two days without a verdict. Every day, Osaru would sit in the lounge outside the courtroom with Brandon's assistant and wait. The jury had been dispatched a couple of days earlier after instructions from the judge. She essentially told them what they could and could not do.

Osaru was getting frustrated by the length of the deliberations. He could not understand why it was taking so long. Was his innocence not clear to them? Did they not appreciate the mental and emotional torture their delay was causing him? He had hardly slept the previous two nights; even short naps were interrupted by nightmares. It reminded him of the night before university-admission results were published several years ago.

College admissions were highly competitive in his country, for the simple fact that there were more qualified applicants than places available, especially for professional courses. The matriculations board conducted a nationwide entrance examination to all colleges once a year. Results were usually published in education offices and college campuses on the last week of July. It was the third week of July, and Osaru was watching the local evening news when the headline screamed the release of the entrance-examination results. A chill went through his spine. This could not be correct, he insisted; the results were not due until a week. Further details confirmed release of the results, which were scheduled for display in designated venues the following morning. Before long his friends assembled. All five of them, including Egbe and his cousin Osato, had studied and taken the examination together. It was the longest night of his life. They considered every possibility, the thrill of acceptance, and the despondence of rejection.

They stayed awake all night and by cockcrow, red-eyed, stormed the local college campus. As early as they were, the crowd was already teeming when they arrived. Everyone was eager to see the list at once; pandemonium, if not anarchy, reigned. To maintain some semblance of order, security officers ordered everyone out of the area and allowed ten viewers at a time for three minutes. It worked reasonably well. Success or failure was palpable, one with smiles or near hysteria, the other with dejection or tears. In the end, Osaru, his cousin, and two friends were accepted, but sadly, Egbe was not. That was a happy ending. The stakes, this time, were higher and different; there was nothing for him to do but wait.

There was a flurry of activities. Brandon had scrambled in from his office. The judge called him in along with the prosecutors. A verdict had probably been reached. It was not to be; the jury merely wanted a portion of the testimony read back to them.

Brandon reassured him that the longer the jury took, the better. It was a sign that they were having a hard time convicting. The word finally came; a verdict had been reached, and all the principal players assumed their positions. The courtroom was still with deafening silence. Osaru, for the first time, started contemplating the possibility of a guilty verdict. He had been adamant about his innocence. He had proffered and protested his innocence to anyone who would listen. He had never considered the possibility of going to jail. Now the imminence of a decision cleared and focused his mind. His denial was over. He had heard all types of horrible stories about jail and was not sure he could survive an extended jail term. By the time the jury walked in, he was a wreck, and only constant assurances from Brandon and LaTonya, his assistant, sustained him. Talking about LaTonya, they had struck a friendship, which in another setting may have blossomed into a romance, but they both knew better.

"Madam Foreman, have you reached a verdict?" the judge asked.

"Yes," she replied. The foreman (forewoman, he thought, would be more appropriate) was one of the jurors who took notes during the trial. The bailiff handed the verdict to the judge; she read and returned it.

Osaru and his attorneys were standing now as the verdict was about to be read. This was high drama; the court system had perfected the process of inflicting mental torture on defendants to an actual form. Why did they insist that a defendant stand to hear the verdict? That was the most vulnerable moment for most defendants, when knees were most likely to buckle. Would the verdict not be as effective if the defendant sat? Osaru never seized to amaze himself, how his mind wandered on trifles in the midst of serious matters. He perfectly understood why Nero fiddled while Rome burned! It was the only thing that kept him sane, the ability to poke fun at himself and see the lighter side of serious issues.

"Count one, possession of narcotics."

"Guilty."

"So says one, so say all."

"Yea," the jurors responded in unison.

The clerk continued, "Count two, conspiracy to traffic drugs."

"Not guilty."

"So says one, so say all."

"Yea," they chorused.

They continued in this robotic fashion till the last charge. He was acquitted of all charges except possession of drugs. As soon the guilty verdict was read, Osaru had gone numbed and tuned out the proceedings. The courtroom moved in slow, silent motion.

"You okay?" The voice was familiar; it was Yolanda's, and it snapped him back to reality. She was there to support him on the urging of Aunt Maria.

Brandon expressed his disappointment with the verdict but pointed out that all but one of the charges ended in an acquittal.

"How many years am I looking at?" he asked.

"Depends, perhaps three to five," Brandon answered. An appeal and a motion to be free on bond pending appeal would be filed, he promised. Sentencing was set for two months hence. That was comforting; at least he would have time to prepare for jail. As they left the courthouse, a bailiff handed Brandon some documents. He flipped through it with a frown on his face getting deeper with each page. It was bad news; the government was filing forfeiture notice on their assets, including properties and bank accounts. Could they do that? he asked. Yes, Brandon replied. A new law permitted the government to seize assets procured with drug money or money-laundry activities.

17

Brandon spent the next couple of weeks filing a dizzying array of motions, injunctions, affidavits, and other documents, many of which were laden with dense legalese like *wherefore, hitherto, supra,* and *infra*. As far as Osaru was concerned, he was engaged in a war he did not understand or speak the language of. They had won a significant concession from the court, that the restaurant business should be unencumbered pending the determination of the government's claim.

Yolanda soon had her fill of legal battles and moved back to her aunt in Arizona. He spent his time tidying up his affairs. Not that it was much. His account was frozen except for a small sum he was allowed for necessities. Even that took countless affidavits declaring why an item was a necessity.

The restaurant, more than ever before, was the center of his life. He threw himself into it like a man possessed. It was the only way to keep his mind occupied away from his imminent confinement. He soon caught up with all his paperwork while supervising and participating in every aspect of the restaurant's activities. Revenues were up and business was good. It was summer. The sun was scorching, but a slow-moving wind made it tolerable. He had taken to walking around the property every afternoon. He liked to soak in the sun. It invigorated him. He would pick up trash as he walked around and stop to watch a bevy of birds that had found a home in the old tree behind the restaurant. They were perpetually in motion, coming, going, and singing. They seemed so carefree. Did they ever go to jail? Watching them reminded him of his childhood and the myths he was told about birds. One of them particularly stood out. *Ahianmwosa* (God's bird) was a common bird in his country. It was a bit bigger and slower than other birds and therefore easy prey for young hunters armed with stones and slings called catapults. These birds were, however, rarely attacked because it was taboo to eat them.

Legend had it that a prominent warrior, Uwa, had boasted that he could shoot and eat God's bird without adverse consequences. As the warrior tracked the bird, it sang the following:

> Don't shoot at me, Uwa!
> For I am God's bird.
> I am God's emissary.
> I am God's disciple of peace.
> Do not shoot at me, Uwa!

Uwa was an obdurate and proud man. He shot and killed the bird despite her entreaties. As he prepared and ate the bird, it continued to sing.

> Don't eat me, Uwa!
> For I am God's bird.
> I am God's disciple of peace.
> Don't eat me, Uwa!

The warrior ignored the bird and had his fill and boasted about his accomplishment. Seven days later, his stomach started to grow and grew larger by the day despite the best efforts of all the renowned medicine men. On the seventh day, Uwa's stomach exploded, and he died. He remembered how, as children, the part of the explosion was accompanied with the listening group clapping their hands in unison to simulate the explosion. How thoroughly they enjoyed it and the hearty laughter that followed. He wondered now whether that story was concocted to protect a relatively big, slow, but graceful bird from extinction, a sort of environmental conservatism enforced by threats of mythical sanctions!

Court was in session to determine his punishment. The court had earlier been informed that he had no prior criminal record, and tests revealed no use or history of drug abuse. To prove this, he had to submit to a urine test. The process of collecting a sample was most humiliating. The detective threw a cup at him and asked him to fill it up in the bathroom while he stood outside the partially opened door! He did that once a week for six weeks.

Four character witnesses from his church testified and gave him a model-citizen testimonial. Mr. Abramson was his usual self, the guy who could make cyanide in honey.

"The defendant has had a fair and even opportunity to present his case, and the jury of his peers has found him guilty beyond a reasonable doubt. The high standard required by law has been satisfied. The defendant is a convicted felon, convicted for possession of drugs. This country is engaged in a chemical warfare. Our cities and neighborhoods have witnessed and continue to witness the scourge that illegal drugs has wrought. Are any of these drugs manufactured in this country? No! They are smuggled in from abroad. These countries are waging a chemical warfare against us. The defendant, an alien, whom we opened our doors to, is a foot soldier in this war. We accepted him and provided him with an environment conducive for realizing his full God-given potential. From all accounts, he took advantage and prospered, but then he got greedy. He wanted more than we could legally offer. He enlisted in the army of chemical invaders. He abused our hospitality and exploited our vulnerabilities. This society was built by immigrants. We are proud of our immigrant heritage, but our forefathers were hardworking people who ate from the sweat of their palms and brows. The defendant is one in a long list of recent immigrants whose greed was limited only by their imagination.

"The state asks for the maximum penalty because there are no extenuating circumstances. The volume of drugs involved demonstrates that the defendant was a major player in the drug trade. If this nation is ever to be taken seriously in its war on drugs, the penalty must fit the crime.

"The devastation inflicted on our communities by drugs has reached epidemic proportions. Serious problems demand serious solutions. The state asks that the defendant be put away for a long time, and fifteen years would be reasonable to satisfy the communities' justifiable sense of outrage."

Fifteen years! Osaru could not believe his ears. Death would be better. How would he survive in jail for that long? This was definitely the end for him. It was Brandon's turn to address the court.

"We reject and object to the prosecution's inflammatory summation and needless hyperboles. Phrases like *chemical warfare* and *alien* serve no useful purpose in a criminal proceeding except to inflame and prejudice the jury against the defendant. This is a criminal matter with predetermined and well-defined perimeters regarding sentencing. The prosecution's request for maximum penalty is unwarranted and unprecedented. There are no aggravating circumstances in this matter. On the contrary, there are extenuating and mitigating circumstances. The defense put forth was not frivolous. In fact, this honorable jury found all but one exculpatory. Vengeance and retribution appear to be the only motive driving the prosecution's request. The purpose of the law is to eschew capriciousness, vigilantism, and lynch mob mentality. Punishment may also be informed by other considerations, like reform, rehabilitation, deterrence, and so forth. There has been no showing throughout this trial that the defendant is dangerous to himself or society. On the contrary, all witnesses, including those called by the prosecution, are in agreement that the defendant is an ordinary citizen with no prior problems with the law. He has absolutely no history of drug use or possession. The defendant came to this country with little or nothing and has made something of himself. He is an entrepreneur and has successfully turned a small restaurant into a thriving concern. At a time when we are promoting family unity and decrying the breakdown of families, should we ruin this young couple by separating them for a period of time? If we do, it will merely be a manifestation of purposeless cruelty. The defense asks the court to take into consideration the totality of the circumstances.

"Despite the prosecutors claim, the defendant was not found guilty of trafficking in drugs or part of a grand conspiracy to inflict chemical warfare on America. The jury has delivered its verdict, and we respect it. We urge that in assessing a just penalty, the jury take into consideration both the rehabilitating and redemptive qualities of punishment—the type of penalty that does not destroy the defendant for the rest of his life but enhances his individual sense of responsibility and a chance to make a better life for himself and family. The defendant has been under indictment for eight months with four weeks of confinement. He has never been confined prior to this matter. In light of all the above, we urge that you temper justice with mercy and suspend our client's sentence with supervision."

This time the jury was swift. He was sentenced to three years in a state jail. He was relieved to learn that he was not going to jail immediately. Brandon had bought him another two weeks of freedom to get ready for prison.

It was his last night of freedom. Yolanda was back in town, and they had been living together for about a week. She would manage the restaurant. Their relationship, which had been hesitant and tentative at first, grew closer and stronger as his departure got nearer. The passion and ferocity took him by surprise. Was he overcompensating for his transgressions? Was she remorseful? Did she overreact? Was it the imminence of their forced separation? Whatever, he was loving every minute of it, and she appeared genuinely pleased too. On this night, however, she was crestfallen and sobbed with her head on his shoulders. Brandon's last-ditch appeal to staying the verdict had been denied earlier in the day. Brandon promised to keep fighting, but Osaru had to report to the authorities in the morning to begin his sentence.

Yolanda sobbed quietly and slowly at first but soon lost control, and like a burst levy, her tears came down in waves, with her body quivering like a snake on fire. When she calmed a little, she stated that she was cursed; anyone she ever loved, she lost. She was afraid to be alone. How could she cope without him? He assured her that he would be out soon, perhaps in fifteen months, according to Brandon, if he behaved himself. Points were given for good behavior, which were then discounted from the term of sentence. That was useful information. He would be a model inmate to ensure quick release, he promised himself. They talked through the night about every possible contingency and how she should handle them. It was a passionate night with very high degrees of gymnastic difficulties.

18

She held tightly to him as the marshal walked into the small and austere waiting room. She had to leave, he insisted; he did not want her to see him handcuffed. Wiping tears from her eyes, she got up, kissed him hurriedly, and marched defiantly away.

Two officers came in to "book" him in. It was a simple process sounding more menacing than it actually was. They assigned him a number, threw a white jumper at him, and took inventory of his personal items. His life behind bars had commenced.

It was the same county jail he had stayed before his trial. A week later, he was woken up early one morning and herded out with other inmates into a waiting van. They must have driven for about two hours before arriving at their destination. It was another jail complete with all the familiar paraphernalia, high walls and barbed wire fences. It was called the diagnostic center, serving primarily as a sort of halfway house for classifying and determining inmates' prison identity and perhaps tame inmates preparatory to prison life. He was marched along with other inmates into a fairly large hall. After uniforms were issued, they were ushered into a dormitory, which looked more like a large warehouse, with no room for privacy whatsoever. Prison life was confirming his worst fears. Was he tough enough to get through it with his sanity preserved? Would he be left with any shred of dignity? He was comforted by the words of a famous political prisoner who once said that he sustained himself, safe in the knowledge that his jailers could take away everything from him except his mind, which only he could give away.

Life in diagnostic was idle and monotonous. The only regular official activity was meeting with prison counselors. His first counselor was a large woman who widened her eyes quizzically when she doubted any response to a question. She appeared particularly troubled by the fact that he had no prior criminal record. This was not the place to lie, she reminded him; she could easily pull up his record if he was not more forthright. She asked all types of intimate questions, including outlandish ones, like whether he had ever slept with another man. Did he prefer men to women or preferred both sexes? What types of unusual sexual activities had he engaged in? Had he ever paid or received money for sex? Was he a violent person? How many fights had he been involved in from elementary school till present? Did he own a gun, use drugs, sold drugs or alcohol? Was he ever abandoned as a child, beaten, molested, or neglected? The questions were endless. He saw three different counselors during this period, and all essentially repeated the same questions. His biggest worry was that nearly every other inmates appeared to be so familiar with the system; obviously, they had seen it all before. They took their loss of freedom in stride, perhaps with a giddiness that was unsettling to him. These young men, many of whom were in their teens and early twenties, were too casual in their attitude toward life. Their world view seemed so warped and disconnected from his reality that he felt a paralyzing sense of loneliness.

His bunkmate, Danny, was a baby-faced kid who had gone astray early in life. He was born without a father because his mother did not actually know. She had multiple partners during the crucial period, all of whom promptly vanished when signs of maternity became obvious. He was her third child. His eldest brother was the only one born in wedlock. His immediate elder brother and two sisters after him were born in similar circumstances as himself. Their mother initially tried all she could to provide for them with some assistance from the government. After her last child, doctors at the public hospital suggested surgical reversal of her productive ability. Two months after the delivery of her last child, she started staying out late and sometimes not returning home at all. On such occasions, they would call their grandmother, Mama Jaunice, who would bring them food and stay around until their mother returned. She would be haggard looking and disheveled and promptly go to sleep. One day she left and never returned. Left to themselves, they called Mama Jaunice, but her phone had been disconnected. His eldest brother, Shaun, then in his early teens, took to the streets, initially acting as a lookout and later as a petty drug dealer and part-time burglar to support them. Neighbors must have called the state authorities as they were awaken one morning by officers of the wards Child Protective Services. Their lives as wards of the state had begun. He never saw his sisters again. He was moved with his brothers from one foster parent to the other until Shaun ran away one day. He was separated from his other brother, and they were moved to different foster homes. When he was fifteen, he ran away to join a gang of boys known as Da Reds. They had no fixed address; their home was a group of abandoned rail coaches in the old rail terminal at the outskirts of the city. Their main occupation was selling drugs and petty burglary. Their vocation was beating up young boys for their jackets and tennis shoes. He recounted with relish several incidents of cruelty they inflicted on their victims, some of which, he insisted, he learned from some of his foster parents, who had administered similar punishments on him and his brothers.

He had been to juvenile detention on two previous occasions. This was his first time in prison. He talked confidently, but occasionally, he would let his guard down, and a frightened little boy would emerge. During such moments of vulnerability, he would yearn for his siblings, his mother, and Grandma Jaunice. He would talk about how he wanted to be a good boy and find his sisters and buy them a big home, and just as quickly, he would snap out of it and return to his granite exterior and threaten fire and brimstone against the snitch who turned him in.

He had been running drugs on the street corner for almost a year without problems when someone else disrespected and dissed him by intruding on his territory. In the drug trade, territorial integrity was defended like national borders. In the ensuing warfare, nothing was left to chance; his gang, which was dominant and ruthless, won a decisive victory.

The challenger escaped with his life and plotted his revenge. In due time, Danny was arrested for selling drugs to undercover agents. He remembered the details of the burst vividly. It was a cold night. He was sitting in his favorite spot at the bar near the intersection. He sat near the door as he normally did so he could observe all movements outside. His customers operated like characters from old spy movies. They would walk past the bar a couple of times, and one of his runners would signal that a buyer was available and that no danger was imminent. He would walk in the opposite direction of his client and exchange his ware for cash in one continuous motion not unlike that of experienced relay runners. This day everything was going according to plan. They had made several sales already; two more sales, and he would be through for the day. He would stay a while with Lulu, the girl he met a week earlier. She was a nice girl, but her mother detested him. The buyer looked the part of an addict, unkempt hair and clothes; the stench of alcohol and cigarette was palpable even before he got close to him. These type of people reminded him of his mother. He hated the job, but he had to make a living. It happened in a flash. As soon as the exchange took place, there was noise and flashlights from every direction. There must have been about twelve men in battle gear and protective vests screaming orders at him. His first instinct was to run, but the intruders closed rather quickly and left no doubt that they would shoot first and ask questions later. He pleaded guilty on the advice of his court-appointed attorney but refused to name accomplices. He got a fifteen-year jail term. If he completed his sentence, he would be in his midthirties when he regained his freedom.

Despite his youth, his knowledge of the prison system was formidable. He walked with a chip on his shoulder, "attitude," he called it. He said he learned from the street that to avoid fights, you had to look tough and convince potential adversaries they would be the worse for the wear if a fight ensued. He boasted endlessly about the tough and terrible things he had done to his enemies or people who dissed (disrespected) him. The level of cruelty he described was bone-chilling.

One day Osaru asked him the question he had been itching to ask but could not.

"Have you ever killed a human being?" Initially, he demurred, apparently caught unawares by the directness of the question. He panicked momentarily, stammered, looked down to his toes, and burst into tears. The arrogant and tough as nails street-smart gangster was replaced with a frightened little boy whom any close observer would have known was always there.

When Osaru first got to diagnostics, he was surprised at the high rate of confession and admission to crimes going on. Everyone told of various crimes they had participated in and gotten away with. The more heinous the crime, the larger the audience. On his part, Osaru continued to profess his innocence until Danny stopped him. He was in a different world now, the kid said, and to survive, he must adapt to its rules.

"It is better for fellow inmates to think that you are a drug baron than an innocent fall guy. Tell them you are a motherfucking Jamaican drug lord, and nobody will mess with you." He was right, because as soon as he started peddling his drug-baron tale, the attitude of other inmates changed from hostility and indifference to admiration and reverence. This piece of prison psychology was to serve him in good stead in the years ahead.

19

Life at the diagnostic unit had a mind-numbing sameness. There was practically no activity except occasional meetings with counselors and watching television. It was a relief at the beginning of the third week when he was moved along with other inmates to the state's prison about an hour and a half's drive from the unit. It was the last time he saw Danny, who was transferred to a different prison. He often thought about him and pictured the frightened little boy with fondness.

The entrance to the main prison compound made no pretensions to elegance; it was an extravagant mix of concrete, pipes, and wire fences. It looked formidable and impregnable. Its stern-looking guards high above the observatory with guns at ready completed the terrifying welcome. They were immediately strip-searched and issued blue jumpers. The warden came into the large reception room to address them. He began by reminding them that they were in prison because they chose, on their volition, to violate societal rules for ensuring harmonious, decent, and peaceful coexistence. Society had therefore decided that until they learned to live within its strictures, they must live outside it. He continued in a voice used to being obeyed, "According to Aristotle, a man is a man in the context of the society. A man outside the society is either a beast or a god. You are outside society as a matter of personal choice, and believe me, you are no gods! At the best of times, life here is hard, demanding, unrelenting, and unforgiving. It could either be hard or extremely hard—the choice is yours. You must decide whether to use your time here for sober reflection, rejuvenation, and reformation for societal acceptance or further wallow in your depravity and degradation. This place is either your penitence or your hell. Take your pick. You are here because you are society's debris. Make no mistakes about it. You will be treated as such. Obedience is expected here at all times. You either give it willingly or, it will be exerted."

It was a tough speech intended to leave no one in doubt that he was the "biggest and meanest dog in town." Osaru looked around to gauge if the speech was as effective on the other inmates as it was with him. Apparently not. They seemed completely unaffected, and some actually carried on private conversations while it lasted. He learned that the speech had become pro forma, worn threadbare by repetition. Due to the high rate of recidivism, most of them had heard it many times over and knew that the warden was not really as hard as his granite exterior would suggest.

It was yet another screening by officers with files from diagnostics in front of them serving as reference. Cell blocks were announced by the captain, and his prison life had begun.

His room was a small rectangle, with a metal double bed attached to the wall. Metal table, chair, and toilet, all attached to the wall, completed the spartan furnishing. Headcounts were at 5:00 a.m. and 10:00 p.m. daily. His roommate introduced himself as Terry and promptly ignored him while concentrating on his reading. The top bunk bed was apparently his since Terry was occupying the lower bed.

Diagnostics had done its job well; now he knew what to expect from prison life. He had resolved earlier to spend his spare time reading all the philosophy books he had always wanted to read but did not have the time or will to do so. Many great works had been written behind bars, no doubt the result of solitude, reflection, and time provided by prison life. He was still not used to prison vocabulary and parlance. For instance, no self-respecting inmate would ever utter the world *jail* or *prison*. No, they were all "incarcerated" in a "penitentiary" because of the perjured testimony of prosecution witnesses, especially "po lice" officers, in collaboration with their incompetent court-appointed attorneys. Despite their confessions to a variety of heinous crimes, he never met a guilty inmate in prison.

Prison offered a little more than diagnostics. There was a library, a gymnasium, basketball courts, a baseball field, Ping-Pong boards, chess, dominos, and a commissary for shopping. Perhaps the most popular room next to the dining room was the television room, which was also the source of frequent arguments and occasional fights. Each cell block had a television room. The general rule was first come, first served. This meant that an earlier inmate or group of inmates decided the channel every other inmate watched. It worked fairly well most of the time but provided occasional flash points for the most heated and foulmouthed arguments in jail. On very rare occasions, it would degenerate into a full-fledged gang warfare, resulting in injuries, some minor, others nearly fatal. He was always amazed at the triviality at the root of such mayhem. On one occasion, it was whether to watch a basketball playoff game or a race car championship. On another occasion, it was which of the competing shock talk shows to watch, the topics being the very illuminating "sisters who sleep with their brothers" or "mothers who sleep with their sons."

Gangs, he was surprised to learn, were a prominent fact of prison life. They were usually organized on racial and geographic lines. The leaders were de facto the unofficial prison government. However, the most influential inmates were the trustees. These were inmates who had served substantial portions of their terms and had earned the trust of the authorities to be included in prison administration. They were given such "delicate" tasks as polishing black boots (bootblack) of prison guards and officers, barb both inmates' and officers' hair, clean the visitors' area, cooking and library assignments. They wore their privileges like badges of honor and usually could make prison life for other inmates extremely unpleasant.

Meals in prison were surprisingly okay most of the time and occasionally outstanding. Breakfast was his favorite meal because he had always been sparse with breakfast. Bread and cornflakes without all the hangers-on was just fine with him.

His roommate, Terry, was decidedly aloof and unfriendly. He seemed to wear a permanent frown, which was made more severe by a scar on his left cheek. He spoke only when spoken to, usually in monosyllables. They had lived together in a space a little bigger than a U-Haul TV box, for almost three weeks, yet he did not know his last name. He seemed to be perpetually lost in thought or reading. He rarely left the room, and when he did, it was briefly to the library to return or pick up a book or two. He received tons of mail, which he studied with the zeal of a finals examination. Out of curiosity, one day, Osaru looked through his reading list and found Hegel, a philosopher he had enjoyed in his college philosophy class. He asked if he could borrow it.

"What do you know about Hegel, young man?" he asked in his grave voice.

"Punishment is the negation of a negation," he answered, one of the few things he could remember about Hegel. Terry looked startled but recovered immediately and launched into a treatise on Hegel. Osaru was impressed with his lucidity and erudition. He could not resist but ask how he got to know so much about Hegel and philosophy.

"Your mind. Developing your mind is the only useful thing you can do here," Terry replied. From then on they were friends and reading pals. The only thing they disagreed about was Terry's adamant opposition to television in any shape or form. He described it in his customary robust language as "a desolate wasteland, an intellectual desert, barren to the core."

Mails were a high point of prison life, receiving or sending one. There were inmate calligraphers and artists who delighted in designing envelops with flowers, obviously to impress the recipient, usually a female of the sender's fantasy. All mails were inspected for contraband, such as drugs, weapons, or money. Content was also scrutinized to ferret or nip in the bud criminal activities.

His first mail was from Yolanda. She was doing okay giving the circumstances. The restaurant was taking all her time, but she was coping. Brandon (his attorney) believed his appeal would be successful, but it could take up to two years. She missed him and hoped to visit as soon as the prison authorities approved. It was not until his second month in jail that she was able to visit. It was a bright Sunday afternoon; he had looked forward eagerly to seeing her. In fact, he hardly slept the previous night. He cut his hair and looked reasonably presentable when he walked into the visitors' lounge. She was sitting in one of the cafeteria-style desks with her back toward him as he was led in by a guard. She was very effusive in her hugs, with beads of tears running down her cheeks. She examined his body as if to ensure everything was intact. The restaurant was hardly breaking even. She was cutting expenses by reducing the sizes of burgers, drinks, and number of staff, but it was a struggle. She was not too certain whether she could make it alone out there. Sure, she could, he reassured her, but she had to stay the course a little longer; the bad publicity would blow over, and customers would come back in droves. They talked on end about everything until a guard ended the visit. She promised to come back the following month. She brought some money for him, but prison rules prohibited direct cash to inmates. The correct procedure, they were told, was for her to purchase money order and send it to an inmate trust fund, which in turn would disburse it to the inmate. So far, he had managed to get by without money and did not anticipate any financial contingency in the near future. The prison commissary, which was the official shopping outlet, was less stocked than a communist supermarket. Thrifty inmates left most of their money untouched in the trust fund; some of them left with a tidy fortune at the end of their term.

He was now fully settled into prison life. His disbelief and utter indifference to his environment had at last evaporated, and reality and resignation settled into. Terry was very helpful in this process. He intellectualized everything. He always counseled that the past was beyond redemption, but the future was still within control and mastery if one prepared now. He always felt inferior in Terry's presence because of his confidence and intellect. He seemed to have answers for everything, not just answers but good ones at that. He often wondered how such a man ended up in jail. He could never bring himself to asking, and Terry never volunteered.

The prison system, to his surprise, ran rather efficiently with occasional disturbances, which was a miracle, given the profile of its inhabitants. The swift, sometimes ruthless administration of penalties for even the slightest miscue was mostly responsible. Guards and trustees were the tip of the ironfisted disciplinary apparatus.

Infringements ranged from the serious—like failure to perform assignments and possession of cigarettes, money, or drugs—to relatively trivial ones like noisemaking and walking behind the yellow lines. A bright yellow line was drawn on the floor of most prison buildings. Inmates were prohibited from walking on a particular side of the line. Some inmates chose to walk across those line for the simple reason that it was banned. He often questioned the rationale for the yellow line. Later, he came to realize that it was an effective imaginary wall that further confined inmates within a clearly defined space.

Punishments ranged from write-ups, verbal reprimand, menial jobs, to lockdown. Lockdown was at the apex of prison penalty, reserved only for the most serious offenses. It meant confinement and absolute loss of freedom for a period. It was dreaded not only because of the obvious loss of freedom but also the maniacal tendencies of its inhabitants. Noise, rants, and shrieks were endless. It was said that insanity was the most probable parting memento from lockdown.

With Terry's influence, who was now a trustee, Osaru got a job as a sorter in the library. Prior to that, he had been working in the shop, making vehicle license plates and street signs. The vanity of some of the personal license plates matched only the exaggerated egos of the owners. He was reading and writing more than at any time in his life except, perhaps, during the month prior to his final college examination. He had been cleared to write his professional accounting examination but was warned that success would not entitle him to practice until he was a legal resident. Every day he would go to the library with Terry at eight. They were usually the first to arrive, not that many inmates bothered to use it. It was perhaps the most underutilized facility in the prison. The quiet, cool, and comfortable setting was a sharp contrast to his college's general cafeteria, which doubled at night as a study room. His college cafeteria was an open semidome building designed with no windows or doors, leaving it very vulnerable to the elements. It was too hot in the afternoons and too cold in the night. The dining tables and chairs were attached together with no backrests. With power supply intermittent at best, candles and kerosene-powered lamps littered atop every table. Studying at general cafeteria was one arduous, unpleasant task. How he wished they had the comfortable and soothing setting of the prison library to study.

He had been in prison for nine months when Terry was moved to a different facility because he was at the tail end of his prison sentence. The night before his departure, he launched into one of his didactic speeches. The will to stay strong, positive, and improve the mind. The importance of communal responsibility. The obligation of fatherhood and so forth. He was going back to politics, from whence he came. This time, he would not be tempted again. He never explained. They hugged, and in the morning, he was gone with a plastic bag containing all his earthly possessions.

His new cell mate, Van, was a muscular young man with a deep, resounding baritone. He was the polar opposite of Terry—loud, vulgar, sloppy, and uncouth. Most irritating to Osaru was that he snored like a windmill when he slept. He intuitively disliked him and tried to keep him at arm's length. After being rebuffed several times, Van decidedly turned hostile and chided him for acting "white" because he was always reading. He accused Osaru of thinking that he was better than everyone else. Well, he had some news for him.

"You ain't better than nobody. You are a damn African! If you were so damn good, why your ass in jail?" Osaru ignored him, which infuriated Van further as he increased the venom of his tirade. Eventually, they settled into an uneasy truce of no war, no peace. They avoided each other as much as possible and argued only occasionally over noise and sloppiness.

Osaru had been sleeping a while when he thought he felt something between his lap and instinctively turned and felt a body on him. He woke with an alarm and pushed with all his might, but the assailant was stronger and pinned him down. The body odor was familiar; he knew it was Van. Osaru kicked and punched furiously to no avail. The intruder pressed on, trying to kiss him. The stench from his mouth was overbearing, and in desperation, he bit the intruder's nose. With a piercing, shrill cry made more sinister by the stillness of the night, the intruder jumped off him. Osaru switched on the light. It was Van, bloody nose and all. He charged at Van and they wrestled, punched, and kicked until two guards showed up. He was relieved to see them as he was now on the receiving end of the fisticuff. In the last couple of minutes before the guards showed up, he had lost his initial adrenaline-induced advantage.

Van was not only a good fighter and pervert but an accomplished liar. He immediately proved his dexterity by turning the tables on Osaru. He told the guards that Osaru had tried to sexually molest him and had bitten his nose when he rebuffed him. Osaru was incredulous. They traded accusations back and forth until the guards found traces of Van's blood on Osaru's bed. They took him away for medical treatment for the night.

At the hearing headed by the assistant warden, Van confessed that he had initiated the assault but that he was not gay. He was driven, he said, by anger at the uppity attitude of Osaru. Van was found guilty and sent to solitary confinement for two weeks. Further, he would henceforth be housed in the gay quarters, which was the nearest thing to a death sentence in jail. Osaru was found guilty of using excessive force to defend himself and was sentenced to menial labor for two weeks. He was also to be classified forthwith as violent. Osaru felt that his punishment was unjustified, but his attorney, a trustee, counseled against an appeal to the warden because the chances of reversal were nil. Further, it could also invite hostility and reprisals from the guards. There was "no upside to an appeal," he concluded.

For the next couple of weeks, he scrubbed and washed the toilets in and around the cafeteria and staff block. It appeared that inmates and guards reserved their most dirty and disgusting habits for the toilet. They practically ignored all sanitary rules and preferred the floor to any other piece of equipment designed for use therein. His written instructions taped conspicuously on the need to use the toilets properly were not only ignored but soiled with wastes. As disgusting as the job was, it was fast and undemanding. It took less than an hour in the morning and another in the evening. He therefore had more time to read and write than he previously had. He wrote letters to his mother and sister and poems for Yolanda. He, however, longed for the end of the two weeks of menial labor. There were days he would step into a filthy toilet and throw up. Thereafter, the stench would stay with him all day. On such occasions, he would forgo food altogether. When he finally completed his sentence, his joy knew no end.

20

He was scheduled to take the accounting certification examination in six months. Most of the recommended study materials were unavailable at the prison library. His request to the public library for books had to go through a bureaucratic maze prior to approval, which invariably meant that most of the books would arrive after the examinations! A trustee named Greg, whose nom de plum was Rocky (because of his muscularity), introduced a guard to him who offered to borrow the books from the public library for a fee, cash only. This was his first contact with the underground economy of prison. He used to wonder how contraband like cigarettes, wine, and drugs got into jail. Now he knew. After several letters to Yolanda, she paid the guard, and he got his books.

Yolanda's letters and visits were now infrequent. She complained in her letters about the burden of running the restaurant, loneliness, and sleepless nights. During her last visit, she talked about selling the restaurant. It took a massive persuasive effort from him to change her mind, but her somber expression when she left bore a foreboding omen.

The envelope looked ordinary enough, but the writing was unfamiliar. He had been in prison for about a year and a half, and his letters were either from Yolanda, his lawyer, or some accreditation body. He tore the envelope open, and a photograph dropped to the floor. It was a baby, a beautiful baby girl who looked quite familiar. She looked so much like his sister. The letter explained the misery. The author was Verma. He raced through its content. She had been meaning to write, but it had been exceedingly difficult to compose an appropriate letter. She would perfectly understand if he hated her and never wanted to see her again, but there was something he ought to know. He had left her with something enduring. She found out after the trial that she was pregnant. If she had been more careful and observant, she would have known much earlier, but by the time it was confirmed, it was too late. If he did not want anything to do with them, she would not hold it against him, but she felt he had a right to know. For her, she had no doubt who the father of her baby was. By the way, her name was Roses. Wasn't she a cute little angel?

He was numbed. He took another look at the picture. The little girl—his daughter!—was staring back at him with a smile and reaching out to touch something. How could he explain this to Yolanda? What did Verma want from him? Although he saw the physical resemblance, he would request a paternity test and take responsibility for her. She, after all, was only a baby. As for Verma, they were through. He must break the news to Yolanda immediately, confess the consequences of his transgressions and await her reaction, which he knew would be dire. He wrote a detailed confession to Yolanda immediately.

It was two Sundays later when Yolanda showed up. She was selling the restaurant and the house and moving to Arizona. Her lawyers would send the divorce papers. There was nothing to talk about. With tears running down her cheeks, she was gone before he could mutter anything.

He mourned for two weeks, during which he wrote several letters to Yolanda. He got a note from the library that he had a parcel. It was a divorce petition. The petition alleged all kinds of cruelty and mental abuse possible. He did not want to go through another trial. He signed a waiver of citation stating his desire not to contest the divorce. In two months, their marriage was over. Brandon worked the terms of settlement, and Yolanda paid a quarter of the proceeds of the sale of the real estates into Brandon's trust account for Osaru's benefit. He never saw or heard from her again.

Through the prison clinic and law library, a paternity test confirmed that Verma's baby was his. He wrote to inquire about her frequently and authorized Brandon to send her a fixed sum of money monthly.

His examination was now only a few weeks away. He had been seriously distracted but was determined to do well. So he buried himself in his studies. The exams were tough, but he had prepared well, given the circumstances. He was optimistic about his chances for success. With the regimented hours required by his exams being over, boredom set in. He applied to the law library to tutor inmates preparing for their General Education Development (GED) certification. The acquaintances he struck while studying for his exams stood him in good stead as he got the appointment even though he was not a trustee and had been classified a violent inmate.

He enjoyed his tutorial assignments and was shocked by the illiteracy rate of many of the inmates. After two weeks, he no longer assumed anything. He had to start from the basics, teaching the alphabet and simple numbers. The eagerness of his students and the steady progress they made delighted him. In no time, his reputation as a diligent and patient teacher spread around the prison, and inmates were scrambling to get a place in his tutorial group. When the first set of his graduates took their tests, he was as apprehensive as they were; their performance would be the barometer for measuring his efficacy as a teacher. He should not have worried. His students did very well, recording the highest success rate in the prison's history. The authorities took notice and made him a trustee, an unprecedented feat for a violent inmate with less than a third of his term served.

The legal officer called one day and informed him that he had been approved for early release but could not be let out immediately because there was an immigration hold on him, which meant he would be released from state prison to the immigration services' custody. Freedom was still elusive. Two days later, he was served with a document called "notice to appear" from the immigration office. The document stated the obvious, that he was not a American citizen but a citizen of Nigeria who was permitted to enter the country on a visiting visa for six months, that he had overstayed the period allowed by his visa without permission. He was therefore summoned to appear before an immigration judge to explain why he should not be removed (deported) to Nigeria. The date and time of the hearing would be communicated to him in due course. It went on to talk about hiring an attorney and change-of-address procedures. While his early release caught him by surprise, he had always assumed since his divorce that deportation was inevitable.

He studied every immigration book he could lay his hands on, but they were all unanimous that he had no relief from deportation. Only marriage to a American citizen could reprieve him. Although, he had an American citizen child, he had not been part of her life; therefore, no discernable hardship on her part could result from his deportation. Further, his daughter had to be twenty-one years or older to file an immediate alien-relative petition for him to remain in America, which was about twenty years hence! Marrying Verma was out of the question. She would never agree, and he could not even bear to think of such a proposition. He knew he had run out of options and had to prepare to go home. He resolved to call Brandon to tidy up his affairs and convert all his assets to cash so that he could be ready to leave at a moment's notice.

Home would not be so bad anyway. His mother, sister, and Ese would make it palatable, he assured himself. The little fortune he had stashed away from Mr. B's adventure would come in handy to establish some kind of business and settle him gradually back into his community.

Ese, sweet Ese, he must write her immediately. He would go back to her like a repentant apostate before an oracle bearing sacrifices and groveling with all the humility he could muster. He last heard from her about a year after he got to jail. He was angry and embarrassed that she knew about his current circumstances. Egbe, his friend—or more appropriately, former friend—had ensured that she did. Ese, always considerate, did not ask why he was in jail but promised to pray for him and hoped God would deliver him. She pledged her love and quoted a lot from the Bible. He had been too angry at Egbe to appreciate the tenderness and maturity displayed in her letter. Reading it now and hearing the words through her voice, he understood why he first fell in love with her. He began to write her, starting from his departure at the airport in Lagos and his refusal to look back because he did not want to see her in tears to the moment he was writing. Concluding, he wrote, "I am sorry to burden you with my woes. But as you can see, I have been chasing the wind, trying to trap a sizable quantity of air in my fist. Needless to add that it has been fruitless. Will you have me back?" It was a copious and exhausting letter. It was cathartic for him and a necessary step to winning her back. He vowed never to let her go again. She never replied, but he wrote every week, scanning the library for every romantic prose or poem to warm her heart.

Osaru was informed that he would be transferred to the diagnostic unit the following day in preparation for release to the immigration authorities. In the evening, he gathered his few possessions together, mainly toiletries, and in the morning, he marched into the waiting van.

Diagnostic was the same old unit with its boring, repetitive routine. The counselors were noticeably friendlier. Their questions were geared toward eliciting the impact of prison life on the inmates and their preparedness for a return to society. They were particularly interested in calculating chances of recidivism. A week later, all the inmates were given a hair cut, money order of the balance of their trust account, and bus passes. His bus pass was later retrieved because the immigration authorities were providing his transportation. He was mildly surprised by the little fortune in his trust account. Yolanda had sent money monthly to the account prior to the divorce, and he rarely, if ever, spent any of it. Talk of a pot of gold in an hour of need. The money would certainly add to his war chest for settling back home in Nigeria. He had been told that he would need every dime of it because of the horrible economic conditions.

The van was tinted, concealing protective iron bars. It was otherwise comfortable with soothing air-conditioning in the blazing sun. There were two guards and a driver in front and four inmates, including himself, at the back of the van. It was a four-hour drive to San Daniz, a sleepy little town on the southern border of America and Mexico. He slept most of the way.

It was very late in the night when they arrived at the immigration detention center. They were huddled into a large hall, where their fingerprints, names, and countries of origin were recorded.

After a rather-tasteless meal, they were given blankets and mattresses and told to have a good night at the hall. Whether the guards intended it or not, it was a cruel joke; mosquitoes ensured that nobody got any sleep, much less a good one. They slapped and fought mosquitoes all night and were relieved when morning finally came, but it had been a baptism of fire.

After four days of feeding them to mosquitoes, the interview process began. Their options were clear—opt for a speedy trial by conceding deportation and getting voluntary departure or insist on a contested trial and stay in detention for as long as six months to two years. What of bail? he asked. Bail will be set at tens of thousands of dollars and must be paid in full, cash only. What was the advantage of voluntary departure? It enabled an alien to leave the country within a specified period after being found removable (deportable) but would eschew the stigma and legal consequences of deportation. To take advantage of this, however, the alien must have the financial wherewithal to transport himself home.

He knew that the game was rigged. Feed inmates to mosquitoes, deprive them of sleep for a week, and offer them the Hobbesian choice of cut and bail or stay and fight. The answer was predictable—every one of them except Juan opted for a speedy trial and conceded deportation in exchange for voluntary departure.

Juan was a native of Mexico, the southern neighbor of America. He came to America when he was twelve as a member of a nomadic band of agricultural workers. His mother had mysteriously disappeared one day from his village without trace. The village elders organized a search party to no avail. He did not know his father. He was told that he died in a hunting accident. His elder sister had married in her early teens and moved to another village. He had not seen or heard from or about her since. His neighbor, Senor Gonzales, prevailed on his son, Chico, who was a migrant agricultural worker in America, to take Juan with him on his next trip.

Led by *coyotes* (human smugglers), they crossed into America using various bush paths and rivers to evade the immigration authorities. Once in America, Chico, Juan, and a group of Mexicans moved from state to state, picking and harvesting fruits and vegetables for farmers. All wages were paid to Chico, who gave them pittance as pocket money. As he grew older, he resented Chico for taking his money. One day he ran away from the farm and hitchhiked to the city. Once in the city, he found a job at a construction site, picking and moving debris. Many years passed, and he had become sophisticated in the ways of the city but longed for his village. At the local grocery store, he met a girl who reminded him of his sister. Magdalena worked at the produce department. Every day he stopped by to chat with her and bring her presents. They eventually became lovers, and she moved in with him.

There were rumors in his community that the new congress dominated by a party out of power for over twenty years had changed the immigration laws, and all undocumented aliens were to be deported at a certain date. They consulted the popular immigration lawyer in their neighborhood, who informed them that Juan was eligible for legalization because of his agricultural-worker background and length of stay in America. Magdalena, on the other hand, would be deported unless she regularized her stay quickly. The quickest means was to marry a American citizen.

Juan talked to his buddy Dale at work. He was willing to help. He would marry Magdalena to keep Juan's love in America. Dale was a lazy chain-smoking teen who should still be in high school, but something had gone wrong somewhere in his young life. The marriage was performed hurriedly, and Dale moved in with the couple to get rid of his monthly-rent headaches. They hired an attorney and filed all the necessary forms.

They were a happy trio for a while, then without warning, Dale's mood changed. He came home late every night drunk, worked only occasionally, and quit altogether after a while. He often demanded money for cigarettes and beer from Juan. Refusal usually invited threats to withdraw his petition and report Magdalena to the immigration authorities. Juan was compelled to take a second job, working as a janitor at a nearby gas station. One night he received a call from the community hospital. Magdalena had been beaten and raped. Dale was the culprit. The police were looking for him. Juan took one look at Magdalena and could barely recognize her. She was bruised and swollen all over with drips taped to her arms. She was still unconscious, the nurses said. He must find Dale. Armed with a knife, his search began. He knew Dale frequented a topless bar near a shallow highway housing a plethora of liquor stores. He found Dale in a drunken stupor, squeezing dollar bills into a dancer's panties. He asked no questions. With multiple stab wounds to the chest, Dale was pronounced dead by the emergency-response team. The local press fed on the case for days, with opinion leaders calling for his execution. The jury was more temperate; they sentenced him to twenty-five years and was released after ten years for good behavior. Juan could not go back to Mexico because he had nowhere to go. Magdalena, upon recovery, sought reprieve from deportation as a victim of violence perpetrated by an American citizen. Her application was denied because she had been engaged in a fraudulent marriage for immigration benefits. She was deported to Mexico after he was sentenced, and he had not heard from or about her ever since. Osaru gave him a few telephone numbers of immigration support groups he had gathered from the library and wished him good luck. Osaru and other inmates who had agreed to a speedy trial were moved to a new and more comfortable facility to await trial and certain deportation.

21

The immigration courtroom was full to capacity with inmates and their families. They were now referred to as respondents. The steady aliases he had acquired in two years amused him to no end—suspect, defendant, respondent, inmate, trustee. The court was tucked away on the fourteenth floor of a tall glass building. The space was obviously too small and looked hastily constructed, almost as an afterthought. Most of the inmates spoke or claimed to speak little or no English. Interpreters were provided, which further delayed the proceedings, although it made for some comical moments. A question would be asked, and the respondent would begin his answer in English before the interpreter interpreted, and suddenly he would remember that he spoke "no English" and shut up midsentence. It reminded him of stories about colonial courts in his country. When colonial courts were first established by the British in the heyday of colonialism, they employed interpreters who were themselves barely literate in English. In one of several anecdotes, an interpreter had argued with a magistrate over the proper name for a charge for a suspect accused of killing his wife on grounds of infidelity. The English Magistrate charged the accused with manslaughter, and the interpreter, sensing a mistake pointed, out that if anything, the charge should read woman slaughter!

The immigration judge looked distressed in his black robe, which hung on him like an unsightly nose hair. The permanent frown on his face completed the picture of a thoroughly unhappy fellow. The cases followed the same pattern. A case is called by the last three digits of the Alien's registration number, which is usually 9 digits. An attorney jumps up, adjust his suit and glasses, clears his throat, announces his name and concede the allegations on the Notice to Appear. The alien would be promptly found deportable, and the attorney would then move for one relief or the other. Voluntary departure appeared to be in vogue on this day as nearly every one of them asked for and got it. Other reliefs like cancellation of removal or asylum were promptly rejected. The proceedings had settled into this well-worn formula when a Nigerian name was called. His waning interest was revived. She was smartly dressed in a navy-blue pin-striped suit. Her lawyer followed the script, conceded deportation, and sought relief but introduced a new element; he argued that she should be spared from deportation because if she were sent back to Nigeria, she would be subjected to mandatory female genital mutilation. He explained that she was from the Rhuoho tribe in Nigeria, which regarded female genital mutilation as a compulsory rite of passage into womanhood. He argued, "Respondent's fear of persecution is not conjectural or speculative but well-founded. Resistance to this practice by respondent would be considered as an affront to the established ways and norms of the Rhuoho tribe, a challenge to centuries of customs, conventions, and usages, the consequences of which could be fatal. This practice is so deeply rooted in tradition and unquestioned acceptance that respondent's resistance will most certainly be visited with very unpleasant consequences." He went on to paint a gory and detailed picture of the mutilation procedure by untrained "witch doctors"— blood, numerous infections, bodily damages, and death. It was nauseating. When he finished, even the stern-looking judge was flustered for a while. The immigration attorney responded with a document put together by the state department. She conceded, quoting from the document that female genital mutilation was practiced by some tribes in Nigeria but that the respondent had exaggerated its practice, that a father usually determined whether to subject his daughter to the practice or not, that there were no communal reprisals for refusal, that most mutilations were done in infancy and not adulthood. And since the respondent was in her twenties, it was unlikely she would ever be subjected to it. The fact that her father or family had not subjected her to it in her infancy provided some evidence that they were either opposed to it or did not subscribe to the practice, that there was no evidence of governmental complicity; in fact, there was evidence that the government had mounted an aggressive media campaign since the midsixties against the practice. She concluded by dismissing the claim as a frivolous afterthought and a last-ditch effort to avoid deportation. Osaru agreed intellectually with the immigration attorney. His experience validated her claims, but emotionally, he was with the young woman from his country. Her attorney's presentation was lucid and the argument ingenious. He was rooting for her. The judge uncharacteristically deferred judgment. He would give his ruling at a later date; he needed more time to deliberate. She had won a temporary reprieve.

Although, Brandon confessed to him that he knew next to nothing about immigration law, they agreed that he would represent him to save cost as he had already conceded deportability anyway. Brandon's primary purpose at the hearing was to wrest one week of freedom for him from the judge to enable him take care of a few odds and ends. As the day progressed, he became a little apprehensive as Brandon, a stickler for time, had not shown up. Osaru called his office twice but was told that he was in court. When he showed a while later, he was dapper as usual and grinning from ear to ear. His appeal on Osaru's criminal conviction was successful, and he had been waiting to obtain a certified copy to present to the judge. He was not quite sure how the new development affected his immigration status, but it could not hurt.

Brandon put up a spirited fight, but in the end, it was futile. The judge concurred with the immigration attorney that he was not being deported for committing a crime but for overstaying his visa. Accordingly, his conviction and subsequent reversal on appeal were irrelevant in the current proceedings. He was granted a week to depart the country voluntarily.

Brandon found him a clean hotel near downtown. It was one of a new genre of small hotels springing up daily in and around downtown Dallas. He would spend the remaining few days shopping; luckily, he was still sitting on a small fortune. Then he would like to see his daughter at least once before he left. Brandon called

Verma's office, but she was on a trip and was not due back until five days hence, which would leave him with barely a day to spare. It was refreshing for him to do the simple things of life once again, like walking into a restaurant and ordering a meal of his choice, waking and sleeping at his convenience, and wearing his own clothes!

His shopping was fast and furious. Most of his old clothes and books had been neatly packed in storage by Brandon, but the clothes were either dated or had shrunk. He needed a new wardrobe. He also shopped for his mother, sister, and Ese. Oh yes, Ese—any beautiful dress he saw, he would visualize her in it and promptly purchase it. At the end of the week he had amassed a sizable consignment.

He had an urge throughout the week to drive to his old restaurant and revisit the root of his personal travail—in a manner of speaking, the scene of the crime. Each time he tried, he turned back at the last moment. On his last evening, he finally summoned enough courage to fulfill his desire. He was stunned by the level of dilapidation and abandonment. While it was true that the business district was never really much to behold, it possessed a certain vitality, vibrance, and color that was unique and inviting. Now it was a drab and colorless block of abandoned buildings with broken windows. Countless graffiti was the only sign of life on the desolate buildings. The restaurant was unrecognizable. It was pale and solemn. The colors on the wall were peeling off in bits and pieces, giving it the distinct look of an overused chessboard. A large chunk of the electronic board on the roof had broken off with a tiny electric wiring dangling down like a noose. How appropriate, he thought; the dangling electric cord was a metaphor of a neighborhood that committed suicide. Suicide was a touchy subject with him. With a heavy heart, he drove back to his motel. The message flicker on the phone was blinking. Verma had called and promised to call again.

His flight was at noon the following day. He had said his good-byes to Brandon and tried unsuccessfully to reach Yolanda to say a final goodbye. With his shopping complete, he retired early to bed. Verma called again, offering her apologies. She was really sad to see him leave, she said. Was there anything she could do to stop it? Only marriage to a American citizen could save him, he replied. Well, if he had told her earlier, she would have married him to keep him around for her daughter. He thanked her for her generosity but told her that he was ready to go home. Yes, she could bring the baby to see him at the airport, but she lived in a different city now; would he pay for the flight tickets for both her and his daughter? He readily agreed and asked if she could bring a camera along. Throughout the night, he tossed from side to side on the bed as his life in America played like a slow silent movie in his mind's eye. Denine's death, he concluded, was the singular most traumatic event, and he was certain that her death changed everything for the worse for him. It was unfortunate that he ceased to communicate with her mother when he went to jail. Someday he would write her and explain.

He lay in the dark, wondering about his mother, sister, and especially Ese. How would they be looking now? Would his mother be old and feeble? Would they be surprised but happy to see him? Would Ese eagerly take him back? Would she still be the sweet innocent girl he once knew or now a wizened old maiden, suspicious of everything and anyone? After all, his people say that a man once bitten by a snake becomes afraid of even a harmless rope. Well, he would do everything to woo her back. How wonderful their lives would be and their beautiful children yet to come. They would have three children; no, four; no, five, three girls and two boys. The girls would look like their mother. Oh, how he would spoil them. He could picture all of them now, laughing and chatting in the swimming pool at the back of their house. Oh yes, the house he was going to build. Nothing magnificent but a home for shelter and comfort, where he would sit in the evenings and recount to his kids his war stories in America. He would have scars to prove it. One day he would take all of them on a vacation to meet their big sister, Roses, who would then be a beautiful tall girl in her own right. Maybe she, too, would want to reside permanently in Nigeria.

When he woke up, he had only two hours to get to the airport. He reported to the immigration officer at the airport, and they checked him in expeditiously. He looked around for Verma but could not find her. Did she change her mind after speaking to him? He hoped not. Perhaps she had come and gone. They were to meet him at gate 27 at 10:30 a.m., but he was about an hour late. He was just settling into his seat when someone tapped him on the shoulders; it was Verma—ravishing and captivating as ever, with a devilish smile playing mischievously on her lips. They hugged, and he picked his daughter up, who to his surprise said "Dada." His heart melted. She was a perfect blend of his sister, Ivie, and Verma, taking the best from both. The height and bronze complexion were Verma's; the elegance, grace, and face were his sister's. They took a lot of pictures until the final boarding call was made. He promised to write and with tears bade his daughter goodbye. Verma stood transfixed as he turned to leave, tears flowing freely down her cheeks. Even little Roses resisted going back to her mother as she clung tightly to him.

As he walked toward the exit, his eyes caught a vaguely familiar newspaper on a nearby newsstand; it was *Nigeria Today*. *Nigeria Today* was a monthly community newspaper published by the energetic and ebullient Ms. Joy Afeni. The newspaper, actually written in magazine style, made no pretensions to journalistic excellence; it was essentially a collage of wire and internet reports of Nigerian news, a few obituaries, and pictorials of social events. Whatever Ms. Afeni lacked in reportorial and editorial expertise, she made up for with unbridled enthusiasm and support for the Nigerian community. Whatever the cause, Ms. Afeni showed up and lent her considerable energy. Her country folks honored and humored her with their patronage. Osaru had been a regular subscriber to *Nigeria Today* before he went to jail. It was the only source of printed information about Nigeria available. The mainstream media outlets covered his country in sound bites and anecdotes; even then, it took famine, war, coup d'état, or other disasters to attract their meager attention. He had been completely cut off all news about his country in the last two years. He picked up a copy of the paper. He would need reading materials for the arduous sixteen-hour flight; if nothing else, he reasoned, it would be a head start for what promised to be heady homecoming. When he would eventually read *Nigeria Today*, he would find on page 3, the society page, a newly married couple, laughing from chin to chin, announcing their newly solemnized matrimony to the world. They were Egbe, his childhood friend, and the girl of his dreams, Ese!

Coming Soon by the same Author

Nothing Now Remains - A Nod to Great Ife

About the Author

Ernest Osaretin Inedonmwon is an attorney. He works and teaches in Dallas, Texas. He received his first degree in law from the University of Ife, Nigeria (now Obafemi Awolowo University), and graduate law degrees from the University of Benin, Nigeria; McGill University, Montreal, Canada; and Texas AM Law School, USA. He is married to Adesuwa, and they have four children. He is a fellow of the International Center for Ocean Development, Halifax, Nova Scotia. He loves traveling, swimming, reading, and reciting poems. He has authored several legal articles and seminal presentations.

CPSIA information can be obtained
at www.ICGtesting.com
Printed in the USA
LVHW042207160919
631220LV00004B/543